'The planet lay like a diamond on the velvet of space. Mark and Paul watched in silence as their craft drew away from it, the hidden fortress, a refuge for those whom the Empire was determined to destroy.

'Ahead was the quest for a woman called Natasha, and a confrontation with the age-old enemy, the wielder of darkness.'

This gripping sequel to *Operation Titan* tells of a daring rescue-bid − on the Empire's notorious prison-camp, Omega 4. Although *Assault on Omega 4* is the sequel to *Operation Titan*, it can be read on its own.

Dilwyn Horvat was born in 1956. He trained as a scientist at Bristol and Oxford, and is married to the singer, Helen Marple.

Dedicated with love
to Helen, Bill Leadbetter, and Chris and Marion

ASSAULT ON OMEGA 4

DILWYN HORVAT

A LION PAPERBACK
Tring · Batavia · Sydney

Copyright © 1986 Dilwyn Marple-Horvat

Published by
Lion Publishing plc
Icknield Way, Tring, Herts, England
ISBN 0 7459 1048 3
Albatross Books Pty Ltd
PO Box 320, Sutherland, NSW 2232, Australia
ISBN 0 86760 836 6

First edition 1986

Cover illustration: Peter Chiang

Printed and bound in Great Britain by
Cox & Wyman Ltd, Reading

PROLOGUE

Behold – an Empire spans the vastness of space. Soaring pride thrusts into the heavens and vaults of power plunge into the deep. The Empire stands astride galaxies conquered by the technology of power.

Listen – a pulse sounds beneath the silence. Travel across the divides, return to the source and discern, whirling at the edge of a galactic spiral, a speck of light infinitesimally small. And smaller still, a pale companion with no light of its own. Just the merest glimmer of reflected glory. And realize, that in this planet beats a heart of darkness that broods over the realms; that has desired to possess them since time immemorial, and that has reached out now through the Empire and rules.

But wait – even as you stand before that place where the beat is strongest and the pulse inexorable can you not feel in the darkness . . . a tremor?

1

The giant star ahead was a pinpoint reflection in the protective visor. Eyes, blue-tinged behind the metallic bloom of the optics, held the image of a sphere with steady concentration.

'Still nothing.' His voice confirmed an earlier judgment. He blinked and looked away from the screen on which their universe was displayed, and half-turned to his companion.

'There's nothing out there and we've got a clear flight in. Do we risk it?'

'It's too easy,' she replied with conviction. 'I think we're being set up.'

'Me too,' he agreed, looking back at the image. As his eyes and the polarizing filters came back into line, the third dimension of the sphere reasserted itself. They were at the origin, triple-zero coordinates, a green speck at the centre of the sphere. Surrounding space was empty, except for the yellow-winking distress beacon drifting steadily inwards as their craft edged cautiously in for the pick-up. The question was whether to commit themselves and go for it.

Easing back in her chair, the pilot relaxed her grip on the control column and inquired casually, 'What do you say we take a look behind that star?'

'Good idea,' the other agreed. 'There's no sense in just rushing in; we can jump out and back with no trouble. If there is anyone out there, it's the only place they could be hiding.'

She programmed the jump and then came back to the alert, grip firm but relaxed on the joystick.

'Ready?' She glanced across. He nodded. There was a momentary pause and then the view ahead exploded in a spectrum starburst as they traversed the light barrier.

The co-pilot blinked. Suddenly the scanner held a small clutch of flashing points, arcing purposefully in toward the centre of the sphere. Reflexes triggered. His fingers moved deftly over the console, eyes tracking the converging flashpoints.

'Three contacts,' he explained. 'Same bearing; thirty degrees, seventy degrees, high proximity, vector plus seven-point-five and rising. Time to engage . . .' He did a rapid calculation, '. . . nine seconds.'

'Going to battle status. Counter measures deployed.' She was talking back over his commentary. 'You have computer priority.' A stream of continuous and overlapping dialogue passed between them.

'Putting scanner on main display.'

A larger replica of the blue-white sphere appeared in space, hanging just inside the flight-deck windscreen.

She watched it for a second, evaluated the scenario, and made her decision.

'I'm going for a modified seven-eighteen,' she stated.

'It didn't work last time,' he countered, then suddenly, 'Engaged.'

The cabin rolled over as she started the manoeuvre. 'That's why it's modified.'

An Epsilon fighter swung towards them across their field of view. Even as he registered his objection, he was paralleling her evasive action in directing the shields and other counter measures. The false images generated around them were drawing heavy fire.

A gut-wrenching yaw, and there was clear space ahead. He took a single glimpse sidewards and his eyes widened as he caught sight of the enemy fighter that had just crossed their flight path now broadside on as if in tight formation, its own nose edging ahead of their own. It was the safest place to be, provided you had the skill and nerve to pull it off.

'Ready to jump,' she said, almost routinely, as if she were unaware of flying wingtip to wingtip with an Empire strike craft. 'Here we go.'

They reappeared within sight of the crippled ship whose distress call they had hoped to answer, and he realized with a shock that she intended to make the pick-up anyway, despite the aggressors hard on their heels. His admiration of her performance so far gave way to amazement.

'You really don't give up, do you?' he commented as he prepared for the coming onslaught. The three predators reappeared from hyperspace uncomfortably close and he turned his attention to management of the defence systems. He did not see their objective approach and drift out of view beneath them, but felt the progress of the docking manoeuvre through the minute impulses of the attitude controllers as they edged into position.

Settling down like a bird on an egg, and shielding it from the destructive energies of the enemy, their craft engorged its inert cargo. There was a delay to secure the smaller vessel and make it an integral part of the larger structure, then they executed a tight turn and accelerated away at an oblique angle to their approach flight path, trailing the pursuit craft astern.

There was a sudden buffeting as explosive warheads struck home against a barely adequate shield somewhere at the edge of their fleeing tail-end profile.

'Stay with it, Mark,' she urged him over his lapse of concentration.

'I can handle it.' He was rearranging the energy distribution to reinforce the weak spot, a task barely completed when the light-drive engaged, and they were flung through a window into oblivion and out the other side.

The tension in the cabin was gone. Mark flipped up the visor of his helmet and relaxed in his chair. His companion exhaled deeply and closed her eyes for a few moments in exhaustion. At last she looked across at him and smiled.

'They certainly aren't pulling punches any more.'

'You can say that again,' he replied weakly. 'On the other hand, you do have a taste for the spectacular.'

'Dead right I have,' she admitted. 'But you can stand the pace. I wouldn't try it with anybody else.'

He was pleased with the compliment. 'Oh, I'm not complaining,' he grinned. 'But I am beginning to wonder what it'll be like really flying with you.'

The cabin roof was tilting upwards and backwards, and she rose from her seat to look out over the simulator.

'Well, I'd hate to think I was ever boring you,' she commented in his direction. 'Sounds like there's a party on out there,' she added.

They climbed out of the flight trainer to the enthusiastic applause of their peers who had obviously seen the whole thing on video. Lindsey and Mark hadn't realized theirs was to be a demonstration flight; they hadn't been told, probably in case it affected their performance. The unrestrained acclaim of the others was heart-warming and slightly embarrassing.

The Green Knight emerged from the control room and met them halfway towards the simulator. They could tell he was pleased before he'd said a word.

'Well done, you two,' he said emphatically. 'You are developing what might be called a fairly creative style.'

He began to walk with them. 'I'm sure you know the Knights are due to select again those candidates who are to go forward at the next commissioning for final training.' He stopped and turned to face them. 'I want you to know I am recommending you both for acceptance.'

It was what they had hoped for, but now that it was happening they could hardly believe it. Their tutor continued, 'We've played games for long enough. I think you're ready for the real thing.' He looked at them in a way that said something of goodbye. He had taught them well, and with one aim: that they should come to this point where they could move on while he remained behind to do the same for others.

'You must begin to think seriously about your vows,' he said gently. 'In the end, it is those realms in which the hardest battle lies.' He paused to impart weight to his words and then turned to Mark. 'On a totally unconnected matter, Mark, I have been told the White Knight is waiting to see you. You should go along there now, and change later. Here,' he stretched out an arm for the helmet, 'I'll look after that. Collect it from my office before coming to dinner.'

Mark exchanged wondering looks with Lindsey. This was completely unexpected and they were both curious what it meant. It seemed she would have to enjoy the congratulations of their friends without him.

The swamp gurgled quietly as Paul Trentam waded through it, disturbing the rotting vegetation. Bubbles of marsh gas rose to the surface at his waist in vague patterns that somehow reflected the movement of his boots sweeping through the plant matter in the depths of the water. At last he felt the bed of the channel rise beneath his feet, and his thighs began to emerge with each step closer to the far bank.

His hands were above head level, each holding a burnished metal cylinder. His arms and face were streaked with mud, the armpits and back of his jacket stained with sweat, the rest of his body soaked in the slime-filled quagmire. He moved steadily, hardly disturbing the water, his eyes alert, watching for something along the bank as he drew closer.

Finally he stood, dripping and stinking, on solid ground again. There was a narrow path leading off into the undergrowth which pressed in on all sides. Not exactly inviting, but there didn't seem to be much choice in the matter. He was beginning to feel distinctly channelled in a certain direction. Somewhere ahead of him, lying in wait, was the thing he was tracking – unless, that was, the tables had turned more than he thought. He doubted that. A Knight learned his skills slowly, but forgot them never. They told him it was still ahead, and not far away. Maybe watching him even now. The taste of sweat was salty on his tongue. He took a last look behind then moved off into the jungle.

Fifteen or twenty paces in and his worst suspicions were confirmed. The track petered out. Nothing moved as he looked round three hundred and sixty degrees. Back in the direction he had come was a single set of footprints; it had covered its tracks well. He was about to return to the river when, out of the corner of his eye, a movement caught his attention. It was a shadow, travelling slowly across the tree trunk to his left, as of a bough bending slowly in the breeze. Except that there wasn't any breeze. A split second later he knew the thing was directly above him – on two accounts. First, because it took that long to calculate from the direction of the sun, and second because it grabbed him at the back of his neck, yanking him up by the jacket collar off the ground. The arm that had snaked down to reach him began to haul him up into the trees.

He felt a rush of anger and humiliation: anger at having been just a second too slow; and humiliation in the knowledge that he must look completely ridiculous dangling ten feet up in the air, legs waving ineffectually. With an effort he controlled his emotion. There was a crisp report, accompanied by a brief flash of light, and he fell abruptly and heavily to earth, together with a clatter of ironmongery. Something resembling a pile of junk landed beside his head and bounced away into the bushes.

He closed his eyes and nursed a sorely bruised elbow. He had landed unceremoniously on his rump to add to the indignities already suffered. When he opened his eyes, it was to the sight of Trainer standing over him, smiling down with genuine mirth. It wasn't often he did so well against Paul, and the Knight's spirits were so obviously soured by the experience that it just added to the comic value of what he had just witnessed.

'You didn't *have* to let it drop me,' Trentam complained with feeling.

'I'm sorry, Paul,' the other said, fighting to keep a straight face and apologizing for the fact that he wasn't making a very good job of it. 'But you did look fairly ridiculous up there. And,' he continued, 'there's no sense in blaming it on the machine. If you will insist on dismembering the limb you're hanging from, what do you expect?' He went over and foraged for the truncated mechanism then picked it up and inspected the broken end where the baraq had severed it from its body. 'Anyway,' he chuckled, 'it's come off a lot worse than you have, I suspect, except maybe for wounded pride.' Then he added more seriously, 'No bones broken, I hope?'

'When the numbness wears off I'll be able to tell you,' the other replied. 'I'm surprised you care.'

'Well, I wouldn't want to be unpopular with the White Knight,' said Trainer. 'He's waiting to see you. The message came through about a quarter of an hour ago, but I thought I'd let you finish first.'

'Thanks a lot,' answered Paul. 'I'd hate to have missed the swamp.'

'My pleasure.' Trainer helped him to his feet. 'I always enjoy our sessions, Paul. You haven't lost any of the old touch. Four out of four isn't bad, and the other three never got near you. I'm impressed as ever.'

The Knight was limping towards the exit and half turned. Trainer could see he was genuinely concerned. 'You really think so?' he asked.

'Positive. There's a good few years in you yet, Paul,' the other affirmed. 'Everyone comes through this department sooner or later, and you're still one of the best. And I don't give praise higher than that on principle,' he said. As they were about to part, Trainer added, 'I don't know what it is you're training for, Paul, but I'd say there isn't a better man for the job. And my prayers go with you.'

3

The broad corridor curved gently upwards. As Mark walked along, he thought he recognized a figure through the crowd ahead and ran to catch up. Sure enough, it was his father. They made their way together and swapped news. When Mark shared the discovery that he was to be recommended for final training, Paul was pleased, but mindful too of the seriousness of the step he was taking.

They arrived at the ante-room and waited while the receptionist announced them, then they were admitted to the office and the White Knight rose to greet them.

Mark was always surprised at how quickly the man dispelled any awe that might have attached itself to his persona. More than any other, he was responsible for the foundation of Ekklesia, and for the continuing function of the Knights of the Church in opposition to the Empire. But nothing in his manner proclaimed the fact. He knew himself to be a man under, as well as in, authority, and the quality of his leadership rose above the failings that might have beset a man who was less aware. More than that, he and Paul were close friends and so Mark knew him from times when he had visited their home, and found him to be immensely likeable.

The two men exchanged pleasantries and then the reason for their appointment was made clear.

'We have received a communication from Tanya,' the White Knight explained, picking up a sheet from his desk. His expression was grave as he continued, 'It is as we feared: Natasha has indeed been consigned to one of the prison-camps.' He handed the paper to Paul who scanned it quickly before looking up.

'Omega 4? One of the terminal work camps?'

'I'm afraid so,' the other replied. 'Nevertheless, Tanya assures me there is reason to believe she is still alive.' He waited for Paul to digest this information. 'On that evidence, Paul, I'm prepared to let you go. You have our full support. The papers are almost ready, I shall outline the mission to a council of the Knights this afternoon.'

Paul smiled, 'I'm very grateful.'

'Oh, nonsense,' the other said, dismissing his gratitude as misplaced. 'After all you've done for us over the years, it is nothing more than a small repayment towards an incalculable debt.'

He sifted the papers on his desk and drew out a sheaf of documents. He turned to the young man and smiled. 'I have just finished looking through your file, Mark. It is a credit to yourself and to your parents. In council today we shall be reviewing the candidates for the next commissioning. That service is to be brought forward to this evening so that the Church may stand publicly with your father and send him out with our blessing. I do not doubt that you will be accepted for final training, together with . . .' He searched the desktop. 'Ah yes, Lindsey Carter.' He looked up, 'I'm sure you are well prepared. But there is another matter. Usually you would transfer immediately to the charge of one of the Knights. Although I would otherwise not advise it, in view of the circumstances I am prepared to recommend that this be your father, for a limited period. Am I right in thinking you would wish to accompany him?'

Mark was perfectly clear in his mind. The speed with which things were happening had surprised him, but there was nothing that would induce him to remain on Ekklesia while his father went in search of his mother.

'I would like to go,' he said firmly.

The White Knight nodded approval. 'Everything will be arranged. I will send word when it is official.' The intercom sounded and he exchanged a few words with his secretary. 'Now I'm afraid I must leave you; the others will be waiting.' He gathered his papers together, walked with them from the room and said warmly in parting, 'I'm looking forward to this evening. You are both very special to me. You will be in my mind constantly until your return, and may the Lord bless you with success in your venture.'

The commissioning was almost over. Towards the end, as the worship swelled in wave after wave of climax, Mark, standing before the massed thousands, had felt as if towers of power were ascending and descending between the hall and the heavens. The chords that ebbed and flowed and sometimes swept across the amphitheatre, so that one part of the congregation seemed to echo another, were vibrant with a life of their own. It was two autumns now since he had watched a line of trees sway in unison in a quickening breeze, and shower down their offering of golden leaves, swirling in the life-giving gusts. So the Spirit moved among the people, shaking loose an offering of praise, alive in the air and falling finally at the feet of the one they loved. Mark could almost feel the breeze. It was autumn now on Earth.

Lindsey was radiant. As they walked back down the aisle, a few paces behind his father, to the antechamber, the first to leave the giant hall, she flashed him a smile and spoke over the singing.

'Come back quickly, Mark; I wouldn't want to get too far ahead of you.'

He laughed at the tease; they were well-matched and she knew it.

As they passed out of sight of the crowd through the exit she reached across, took his arm and faced him long enough to say, 'I'll be thinking of you all the time.' Then the seriousness broke and she smiled, 'Just like almost everyone else here tonight.' She paused as if composing something else, and then looked round quickly. 'I've got to go and find my parents; I bet they can hardly stand the excitement,' she said. She pulled away and made for the stairs to the upper circle, turning just for a moment. 'I'll see you soon,' she added.

He called back a reply and then she was gone. So now the preparation was over and it was just him and his father. Just the two of them and − a job to be done.

4

Ekklesia, jewel in the crown of the system they were leaving, lay diamantine upon the velvet of space. Mark and his father were silent and watched as their craft drew away from the stronghold; hidden fortress of the Knights of the Church, and a refuge for those whom the Empire would destroy. They themselves had reached Ekklesia only two years earlier, fleeing an Empire Star Fleet with fugitives from Titan. Now they were leaving friends behind them. Ahead was the quest for a woman called Natasha, and a confrontation with the age-old enemy, the wielder of darkness. Even now he was stirring; guessing their purposes, probing their defences and, unknown to them, selecting a champion to oppose them. But, warriors though they were, they too had a champion. They would fight well, and they would not fight alone.

On the planet to which they were returning, and in the city that was their destination, there was a man upon whom the attention of the enemy came to rest. And as the action on the streets unfolded, there was a grim satisfaction in the heart of darkness and the choice was made. Here was a champion worthy to serve.

Devo stubbed out the cigar against the brickwork and leaned back into the alcove against the wall, merging with the shadows. Across the far side of the street, the car with dark windows waited patiently, hovering two feet off the ground, one door open. The rain in the gutter on its way to the sewers formed a wake around a small tin can. When the neon sign sparked, the rim of the can flashed at him from the shadow of the vehicle.

The watcher glanced up and let his gaze travel down from the rooftop advertisement to street-level and the display window fronting the building. The woman in the window, wearing a cute costume, courtesy of the management, returned to the easy chair on her side of the pay counter as the man she had been talking to, who had arrived in the car, went upstairs.

Unseen in the darkness, the attitude of the one who was waiting changed. Suddenly it was no longer the rain sounding in his ears, but the voice of experience whispering that the deal was being clinched. In a room somewhere, money and merchandise was changing hands. And if he wasn't much mistaken, the stuff would be coming right back down those stairs any time now.

True to his prediction, a few minutes later the man reappeared, descending the red velvet carpet of the staircase briskly, purposefully, carrying a small black case in his right hand. He passed the receptionist without a nod in her direction and swept past the doorman, who was standing on guard just inside the entrance lobby. As he stepped out onto the pavement, and turned right towards the vehicle, the other made his move.

A challenge rang out across the street, backed up by an ugly weapon levelled in the courier's direction. The man with the suitcase ducked towards the car, lobbing the goods in through the open door. He had covered half the distance when he was caught by the blast from the gun and thrown back through the plate-glass window into the lap of the receptionist.

The car came to life, engines roaring, rising as the door closed. The gun barrel dropped a little but the second shot missed. Devo swore; the neon sign lit and the can winked at him from the gutter. He fired twice and fast, so that the second was an echo of the first, and was rewarded, on the last, with a pillar of flame that shot up to engulf the rising vehicle. There was a secondary thunderbolt as the car exploded, showering hot metal onto the street below.

Devo stepped out into the open and surveyed the wreckage steaming in the rain. He looked at it and summed it up with a curse. He had just cut his commission by fifty per cent. There was movement in the window and he walked over to take a look. The woman heaved the man off her and he slid to the floor. Devo noted with satisfaction that the wound was exactly where he had intended to place it – he would live. By the man's side, inches away from his right hand, were two things: a small and nasty weapon, and a burst sachet of white powder emptied onto the carpet. Of course; a little something for personal use. Funny how harmless the drug looked in its neat little polythene bag.

'Well now . . .' Devo smiled humourlessly, 'seems

20

you'll talk with the commissioner after all. Too bad you didn't reply to his first invitation, now isn't it?'

The woman was backing away slowly towards the door. He looked up from the man on the floor and encouraged her on her way quietly.

'That's the best move you've made all night, lady. I see you realize you're surplus to requirements on this occasion.' His voice hardened. 'When you get through that door, you run. And I suggest you get well clear of this. Nobody likes witnesses.'

She bolted. So that was his good deed for the day. A quick mental calculation confirmed his earlier judgment. This wasn't the best piece of work he'd ever done. After he offset the cost of the fireworks – over a pound of really rare explosives – he'd be lucky to make a profit. And then there was the commissioner to explain things to. He wasn't going to be pleased.

5

The starburst detonation expelled him into a bright, cold world. Mark spun in the darkness and the constellation of lights, spread out below him, tumbled over and over. He flung out his limbs into the nothingness, bracing himself against the cold night sky rushing by. Then he righted and reached for the ripcord. His fingers closed and tugged. The pack tore open and an invisible canopy billowed open above him.

He descended, swinging gently at the bottom of his lifeline.

The city stretched to the horizon, a plexus of fine bright flashpoints against a darkened backcloth. He began to pick out floodlit landmarks, and the path of the river with its bridging filaments of streetlights. He started to control his descent, gliding towards a patch of parkland some distance to the left. He was entering the air traffic lanes, thick with commuters earlier in the day but now almost empty. Occasionally a car spiralled up towards him before turning away in another direction. Over the south bank, buzzing with nightlife, firefly aircars hung above the city ferrying the ultra-chic inhabitants of the city between distractions. The skyline rose around him as he headed towards his fast-expanding target. Something – a tree, a building? – flashed past uncomfortably close; then he was rolling on the turf and hauling in his paravane.

The sounds of the city burst in upon him as he removed his helmet. Stepping out of his flying suit, he looked around for any notice of his arrival. Some bushes nearby were the ideal hiding place for the loose bundle and he stuffed it amongst the shrubbery, pushing the helmet down on top. Then, satisfied that his arrival on planet Earth had not attracted any unwelcome attention, he began the trek to the apartment where they were all to meet; a walk of perhaps a mile and a half through the streets.

Mark was on the lookout for his father, who would be threading his way through the crowds in the same direction; he must have come down nearby. But there was no sign of him. It was perhaps reassuring that from the moment his own tube had blown apart, disgorging him into the night, they had been invisible to one another. It strengthened the hope that they had come in under the very nostrils of the Empire without detection. The spacecraft that had dropped them high over the mid-Atlantic was long gone. The skin-tight capsules that had brought them in, entombed like mummies, over the south of England towards the capital were fragmented and dispersed.

As he thought back over their three-stage descent, another part of his mind was matching his progress to the map inside his head: past the domed grandeur of the Albert Hall, the quiet of the University science departments, their basement libraries all but deserted, and on into the buzz of life at the heart of the city.

The capital was a glittering showcase of all that the Empire claimed to provide. Miraculously spared through the tortuous conflict that was the Empire's birth, it had become the symbol of the new age. Its bigger brothers – New York, Los Angeles, Mexico City – had all attracted too much attention, but somehow, London had slipped through.

As Mark made his way further south, he found himself surrounded by the citydwellers – beautiful, rich, successful. But the life of the city was built on the bones of the dead. A previous population, dispatched by a single neutron bomb, had stepped aside to make way for the Empire's favoured, the generation of survivors who at the right time chose to be on the right side.

Mark arrived without incident and in good time. The Georgian terrace adjoined a secluded garden square, already flourishing with a new growth of shrubs and saplings. It was hard to believe these too had sprung into existence, pre-packed and imported, less than a lifetime ago. Everything that lived, and moved and breathed in the vast metropolis had arrived just a few years earlier.

He pressed a button on the panel, answered the intercom, and heard a bolt click back on the door. He entered the vestibule and closed the door behind him. The hallway was warm and carpeted. Stairs led up to the top floor and a door opened to admit him as he arrived. A small reception area opened into a comfortable lounge. He knew neither of its occupants – a middle-aged couple. They, for their part, greeted him warmly. Introductions were hardly completed when the intercom signalled again and the woman who had admitted him rose, exchanged a few words over the line, and gave entrance to the new arrival. The three waited in silence until the second visitor had slipped into the flat and the door had closed behind him.

'Well done, Mark,' Paul complimented his son as he entered the small lounge. 'Any problems?'

'No; how about you?'

'Fine . . .' a pause to look at his watch; 'Well, that's a good start. No sign of Tanya I suppose?' he enquired of their hosts.

'Not yet. But we didn't expect to hear from her again after the first call. She'll be here soon, I'm sure.'

At that moment, a door leading to an adjoining room nudged open and a beast emerged whose looks shocked the two newcomers. It was a dog – large, and powerfully built around a heavy frame. There was something ungainly in its movements, but the thing that arrested their attention was its wicked expression, arising in part from an ugly deformity marring the right side of its face. The creature settled in the far corner of the room, from where it surveyed the two strangers with an unsettling sidelong glance.

'Don't worry – Phoenix looks menacing but won't hurt you,' they were reassured. 'She belongs to Saatchi. She'll be out in a moment.'

The name registered in Mark's thoughts: their guide. What he had heard had intrigued him. And they were all depending on her. He looked at his watch, more from nervousness than a need to know the time. His father was taking in details of recent events from the couple who had been involved in preparations for this rendezvous over the past few months.

The door to the inner room opened again and Saatchi emerged. Mark was immediately struck by two things: her appearance and her bearing. Her features showed evidence also of the dirty war that had been waged across continents the world over. In her case, the effect had been confined to her eyes, but it rendered her just as striking as the dog at her side. Neither Mark nor his father succeeded in concealing his astonishment, though both tried.

She was unperturbed, however, and it was this that made the stronger impression on first meeting. There was a quiet strength about her that inspired confidence, and suggested she would rise to any situation. In the conversation which took place, while they awaited Tanya's arrival, Saatchi spoke little and listened attentively. Mark felt that almost any opinion he might form about her on this first encounter would probably turn out to be an underestimate. She seemed younger than he had expected, though of course nobody could be sure. Still; he'd guess she was around sixteen, which made them contemporaries.

The next half hour passed slowly in waiting and conversation. Paul, Mark and Saatchi were like sprinters on the blocks, living the instant before the pistol shot. When the signal came, they were ready. Mark felt a rush of relief as he recognized Tanya's voice over the intercom.

She greeted them with a hug. It was an emotional reunion, the more intense because of the urgency of their situation. Mark was shocked again by Tanya's exact likeness to his own mother, Natasha: a mother he had not seen for more than eleven years. Their traumatic separation at the Empire's hands had left him only nightmare memories of a woman whose identity he had not guessed, and which his father had hidden from him for safety's sake.

25

But his first encounter with Tanya, two years previously, and still at that time in the Empire's pay, had catapulted him into an awareness of his tragic past, and begun the search for Natasha, his mother – Tanya's twin – that had brought him now back to Earth with his father, fugitives both.

The fact that Tanya was again wearing the black Security uniform reminded him even more forcibly of that previous meeting and his present status, as someone the authorities would dearly like to lay hands on for what he knew of the Church on Earth and on Ekklesia.

Tanya gave them a brief outline of their venture. Maps were laid out to complement the explanation; maps that had been redrawn since the war – of the new South of England, heritage of the warmongers of past decades.

The finger that came to rest near the centre of the sheet was the first indicator of the scale of the problems facing them. Their projected assault would take them deep into the battle-scarred badlands. Somewhere in those arid wastes was Natasha. Or at least, she might be there; and so might Ghia, Saatchi's brother.

Saatchi's contribution was equally sobering. When she had appeared out of the wasteland nine years ago, she had brought with her the fear, and the memory of her brother taken by the Sentinels. These Sentinels, guardians of the camps, mechanical henchmen of the Empire's rule, stood between them and the ones they sought. Although he knew they were prepared, the thought crossed Mark's mind that no amount of research guaranteed all the important facts were known. Their intelligence had better be accurate, otherwise all hell could break loose.

The briefing lasted five or ten minutes. But as the session went on, with more and more interruptions and questions, Tanya seemed to become suddenly uneasy and anxiously broke off her explanation. The rest would have to wait. They collected the three back packs and gathered in the small entrance hall. Their hosts voiced a prayer into the darkness, and Tanya was on her way back to the squad car, whose distinctive black lines and Security number plates could be relied upon to cause alarm in any residential district, and which she had therefore parked a discreet distance from their terrace around the square. One by one, at intervals, they followed.

Standing waiting his turn, Mark found himself distracted by the asthmatic pant of the dog's breathing somewhere behind him. He caught snatches of something like whispered conversation from Saatchi; presumably to calm the animal. Then the door opened and he felt a gentle pressure on his shoulder — almost a gesture of goodwill — to send him off. He made his way downstairs and out into the open.

The car had risen to the exclusive lanes of the diplomat levels in which they were now travelling. Airspace was almost clear and they were cruising at an exhilarating speed uninhibited by traffic. Tanya, relaxed now and guardedly confident, supplied them with as much detail as she knew.

The Omega camps were part of the Empire

administration's 'grand plan' of reclamation – making the land which had been ruined by nuclear war usable again. It was not one of the more publicized angles, but vital nevertheless. The vast tracts of land to be cleared, together with the size of the available labour force, had seemed to go naturally hand in hand; and those who had spoken out against the Empire's rule had thus been put to good use. The dissident population was ideal fodder for the dirtiest work of topsoil clearance in the worst hit areas where success was hardest won and the death toll highest.

Central records, accessible to Tanya as a member of the Security forces, had enabled her to trace Natasha as far as her embarkation on a 'resettlement' convoy to Omega 4 almost two years previously. Naturally, there had been nothing since. The periodic interrogation of political prisoners in the camp seldom turned up anything new; there were no recent entries in the file. The only source of hope was that the file had not been closed, and Natasha might therefore still be alive.

There was nothing on Saatchi's brother. Survivors scavenged by the Sentinels from the badlands around the camps seldom had identities that could be traced back to pre-war days. Usually they remained nameless, a statistic on the workforce. Records did show a number of such gains at Omega 4, but there were no biographical details. And nine years was a long time to survive in a terminal work camp. Of the four of them, Mark reasoned, Saatchi's spirits must be lowest. If it didn't amount to a betrayal, he would have said there was no chance of finding her brother; but he silenced the thought. She was certainly determined, he admitted, looking across in her direction. As for that dog of hers . . . When he looked down he found its gaze fastened on him, and there was a low growl in its throat. He exchanged glances with Saatchi and she quietened the beast with a word. He turned away to pray, rather than worry about this strange alliance upon which their success depended.

Saatchi was tense, and this mood was mirrored by the dog at her feet, whose hair bristled at each turn of the vehicle.

They were travelling now over the outskirts of the city, and Tanya was guiding the car down to less conspicuous levels. The streets below were featureless and suburban. Tanya spoke without turning.

'When we reach the green belt I'll have to use my Security pass to gain access. There shouldn't be any problem, but try to look relaxed. If the guard gets suspicious and wants central verification then we might be in trouble; they're bound to wonder why I'm taking the squad car rather than my own.'

'That had occurred to me too,' Paul said. 'But I supposed you had a reason.'

Tanya nodded, 'Reason is, in this buggy he's less likely to ask questions in the first place; for instance, why are we going into the green belt at all. As far as he knows, we're the wrong people to be unpopular with. In this uniform, you're practically immune; at least, that's the theory. And it meant we could use the fast lanes back there, which might have been important.' She gave Paul a sideways glance. 'There are also one or two extra facilities on this model . . . Anyway, as I said, I don't anticipate trouble.'

They travelled on in silence, skimming along now at street level. Streetlighting was poor and all four stared ahead into the darkness at the limit of the twin beams. In the distance, a loose cluster of lights, centred on their horizon, appeared to be drawing closer.

'That's the terminus dead ahead,' Tanya announced. 'Beyond that, it's open country.'

Minutes later they joined one of the approach roads descending gradually to the underground levels and the checkpoint at the heart of the building.

At the far end of the tunnel, the car emerged into the cavernous underground complex of the terminus. They were shepherded towards one of the row of checkpoints and drew level with the automatic pass controller for their lane, just before the barriers.

The window of the car slid down and Tanya inserted her card into the machine, then pressed her palm briefly against the opaque panel beside the slot. A yellow rectangle lit up with the word 'verifying'. They waited.

Across the other side of the building, several container vessels loaded with agricultural produce were passing in the other direction; tomorrow's fresh vegetables for the city they were leaving. Several of the vehicles were parked and drivers were chatting whilst the rest were given clearance.

In the control room above the row of checkpoints were several uniformed figures; one was watching them without much interest between bites of a sandwich and an apparently humorous exchange with a second character out of sight.

When the security guard looked down at the console on his left, Tanya murmured to Paul, 'I think he's checking us out now . . . Seems to be taking his time, but looks fairly relaxed.' Her eyes followed the movements of the chewing one. 'Now he's put his sandwich down.' Her hands moved over the dashboard, touching several of the controls. She was straining with all her sensitivity for some indication what to do next.

'I don't like it . . .' her inflexion was quite definite now. 'He's talking again, but I don't think . . .' The next second it was as if a voice sounded inside her head, with the single word 'Go!'. She reacted in an instant, so that her fingers hit the buttons a moment before the security guard's unseen hand closed on the lever that would seal the exits.

Mark's neck whiplashed back as the vehicle powered forwards. There was a yelp of pain and fright as someone's boot caught the dog at their feet. An explosive sibilance sounded across the complex and the barrier ahead dissolved into light and flames. The car slewed across the tarmac towards the closing exit portal, entered at an angle through the narrowing opening, straightened and accelerated up the ramp to the outside world.

Saatchi had been flung bodily across the passenger compartment and her dog was struggling to get out of the seatwell where she had received a sudden trampling; and creating an awful din.

For a while, all was confusion.

'Just stay down!' Tanya commanded as chaos subsided.

Mark was squashed obliquely against the side window. In the rear screen he could see a distorted reflection of the display panel at the centre of the dashboard. The speckled lights of the terminus complex swung across the image, sucked away into the middle distance behind as the car streaked into the night sky.

'Here they come . . .' Now the tones were calculated, urgent. A cover slid back from an array of winking lights whose significance could only be guessed in mirror image. Mark saw Tanya's hand over the console, fingers curved and poised. And he distinctly heard her whisper 'Please, Lord,' as she gauged the instant.

He heard his father's voice, sharp and urgent, 'Wait; make sure they aren't . . .'

Tanya was oblivious of everything except the screen and the projectiles homing in on their vehicle. Paul's objection came too late.

Again there was the explosive spitting sound, and a second and third volley. Twin detonations rocked the vehicle and they were bathed for a second in an intense white light. Then the car banked steeply and accelerated off at a tangent. The tension subsided and Mark breathed more easily as Saatchi lifted her weight from him and regained her seat.

They were all shocked by the sudden explosion of violence. Only Tanya had realized what was happening and why she had to respond so decisively. She was shaking, and her voice faltered slightly as she explained.

'Sorry there was no time to warn you back there,' she said. Then she continued more steadily, 'The guard was talking to someone else and I didn't know who. But whoever it was told him to check us out more carefully. And the instant he decided to keep us there for a more thorough clearance, the Lord told me to go. Those exits were sealing before we even moved. I don't know what made him suspicious of what we were up to, but I do know that if I hadn't gone when I did we'd have been trapped and helpless.'

'And those two that came after us?' Paul asked.

'They weren't manned. They were small, fast and tracking; and for my money that makes them heat-seeking missiles. The car doesn't exist that could overhaul us at the rate they were coming.'

There was silence as Paul understood, and realized what he had nearly done in questioning Tanya's decision to shoot them down.

'I'm sorry. I almost got in the way.'

She glanced across at him. 'It's all right; you couldn't have known.'

It was becoming clear that they would have to work as a team, each with a unique contribution to make.

Eventually Saatchi spoke up. 'What happens next?'

'First thing is to find out where exactly we are,' Tanya replied. 'We'll have to get well above the tree line for terrain matching. Once the computer tells us which bit of the country we're over at the moment, I'll know which direction we should be heading. We might as well take a straight line from here to the edge of the badlands. As long as we stay clear of the main routes, and fly low over open country, I don't think they'll be able to pick us up.' She thought for a minute. 'Is everyone all right in the back?'

'I caught my neck and it's sore,' replied Mark, 'But I think it's okay.'

'We're fine,' said Saatchi. 'Phoenix is quiet.'

'How long before we clear the green belt?' Paul asked.

'At this speed, about half an hour,' answered Tanya. She checked the video display. 'All looks quiet; let's see where we are.'

They settled back into silence and wondered. If Tanya hadn't been prompted as that unseen hand moved against them; or if she had failed to respond, the battle would already be over.

7

The room breathed to the strains of improvized jazz. In a corner, the video sent a cross current of dialogue that submerged with the swell of tenor sax, then reasserted itself as the melody ebbed. The lights were dimmed, and the flickering screen held sway. In the shadows, random flecks of red and blue etched out the decibels of the soundtrack. Ageing compact discs lay against the music centre – American imports, rare mixes and bootleg originals. Devo was a connoisseur.

He was relaxing; reclining in the easy chair near the centre of the room, feet up on a low table in front. Beercans littered the floor. One or two had found their way almost to the bin across the far side of the room; others had stayed closer to home. Smoke from the very best cigars hung in the air, hardly drifting. And the very best ash fell from the glowing butt to the ashtray on the floor, or thereabouts. The taste of the smoke was cool and mellow on Devo's tongue; the taste of the beer also pleasant in its own way, though probably the other cans needed to go back in the fridge a while. He was wondering whether to eat, which meant going out to the kitchen or take-away; or sleep, in which case he could stay right where he was. And he was just coming round to the first course of action when another option presented itself. He could answer the phone. At first this looked like an outsider, and he let it wait. When it kept on calling he decided you never knew and reached out for the remote control.

'Well, well, well,' a smile broadened on his face, 'Commissioner Lawson. How pleasant to see you again after all this while. It really is . . .'

'So I'm sure,' replied the other. 'It's always good to renew old . . . friendships, shall we say?'

'You're so right,' Devo replied. 'I was beginning to think we weren't buddies any more. And now, here you are; just shows how wrong a man can be.' He sucked long on the cigar and exhaled lazily.

'I'd rather not talk to a smoke screen; if you don't mind.'

'Why of course, Commissioner. Things are a little hazy in here, now you come to mention it.' He play-dispersed the fog with a few waves of the hand and sat forward in the chair. 'There now; you have my "full and undivided attention" as they say. Maybe there's something on your mind you want to tell me about?'

'I have a little job for you, if you're interested.'

'I thought maybe that was it,' Devo replied, pointedly easing back into the chair again. 'I'm all ears . . .'

'One of our people has absconded and seems to be headed for badlands to the north; carved her way out of Slough terminus and made off across the green belt. She had three passengers. We think they're making for the Omega camps and would like you to bring them back. And this time we'd like you to try very, very hard to make sure they're still alive when we get them. Just for a change,' he concluded with undisguised sarcasm.

'Tell me, Commissioner,' Devo came back, 'am I in your good books or your bad books at the moment? Sometimes it's a little hard to tell. I've been getting some really fine assignments recently, seems to me.'

'I'd say you were doing fairly well,' the other levelled. 'But there are other people we can buy . . .'

'And you're asking me first. How touching. Incidentally, Commissioner, how much are you offering for this little joyride?'

'Two hundred,' the other offered; though the attempt to make it sound final was unconvincing.

Devo flicked some ash. 'I'd rather rob the bank round the corner,' he answered.

There was a pause.

'Three.'

Another silence.

He stirred himself. 'Commissioner; it occurs to me that I'm really fairly busy just at the moment,' – waving his cigar to indicate the room around – 'I have to fix something to eat, and take a bath; you know how long these things can take . . .'

'All right; three-fifty. I have other calls to make. Don't waste my time.'

Devo breathed out a stream of smoke in the other's direction, and swore under his breath. 'I'll take it. Call you back for details once I've got things moving.' He ceremonially laid the still smoking cigar butt in the lid of his beercan, and allowed himself a last impertinence.

'Incidentally – you wouldn't be bearing any grudges since that little party of yours, would you?'

Lawson grimaced. 'The pleasure was all yours – from what I heard. I don't know why I bothered to save your neck.'

'Why Commissioner . . .' the other laughed and spread his arms, 'that's what friends are for.' Then he added quickly, 'Pass on my regards to the lady in question . . .' and cut the line before the other could reply.

He chuckled as he rose from the chair. Maybe he shouldn't have said that. Still, on balance, the Commissioner still needed him a lot more than the other way round; he could get away with it. He thought about changing his jeans – shame to ruin a good pair – then decided not to bother. He turned up the lights and went over to the locked chest against the far wall. He needed something chemical to sober up and one or two toys for the ride. Then it looked like being a take-away after all.

Tanya and Paul were silhouettes on the skyline. They were standing close and staring ahead into the darkness. From their vantage point on the crest of the scarp, the Oxfordshire basin stretched out into the distance.

The darkness was discomfortingly complete. There was hardly any moon, and the longer they looked, the more uniform the greyness seemed to be. The city they knew to be spread out before them in the middle distance was wreathed in death's dust. The kiss of dawn would leave her beauty sleeping.

There was a low fog, and the night-glasses were useless. Paul lowered them and turned to answer Tanya's question.

'Well, yes, I suppose I am partly afraid,' he

admitted, searching her expression. 'Afraid to find out after so long. Aren't you?'

She nodded. 'There were so many broken families after the war, I sometimes wondered why God kept me hanging on, thinking one day I'd find her. Somehow I could never quite give up. And then when she turned up on the transporter through Titan to Earth, and I saw her name on the list, I knew it had to be true. When I found you again, I could see it all coming together and I knew he'd had a plan through all the years of silence. Waiting; just waiting.'

'The last two years have been hard sometimes,' Paul admitted. 'Once you told me Natasha was still alive, Ekklesia was the last place I wanted to be. I just wanted to get back here and find her. The waiting wasn't easy. Sometimes I stayed up all night asking God to get things moving and it seemed like he wasn't listening.'

'Come on,' she encouraged him. 'Stir yourself, Paul. He cares more for Natasha than we do put together, and he isn't about to ruin it now. You know that.'

Paul was surprised and smiled sheepishly. 'You know, Tanya, sometimes I really appreciate you.'

'That's just the way it ought to be . . .' she replied quietly. Then she shivered in the chill wind and turned back to the car so that he did not see her expression.

'Let's go and find her.'

Devo was doing what he liked best: cruising. His belly was full – he belched his appreciation of Chinese cuisine – and the music was vibrant in his dream machine. The city was a blur; the speed, effortless. The engines were barely audible. When he reached down and touched the main drive manifold it was cool and vibrationless. 'Barely turning over,' he told himself.

He always flew fast and low. A casual disregard for safety and the law meant it was pure pleasure to tax his skills in traffic at night time. But this night he jetted up to clear sky and let the power loose.

The car was flying itself and he chewed on his cigar with infinite satisfaction. With his hands off the controls she went straight as a die. She was a precision machine, custom built. A man of his modesty naturally shied away from the word genius; but at moments like this it did come naturally to mind, and he was prepared to make an exception.

'A rare talent, Devo,' he sighed. 'Yes indeed, a rare talent.'

He had every reason to feel pleased with himself; and indeed passed much of the time in that very attitude. But deep down, there was a worm in the woodpile. 'Why do I tolerate fat fools like Lawson,' he thought, 'if I'm so smart? Why does my comfortable little life depend on such pathetic little men?' It was demeaning. An alternative presented itself to him – the memory of a woman who had made him feel vulnerable in a way he'd found hard to admit. Lucia had seen something in him beyond a rather nasty tool of nastier men. And she had thought that he could leave it all behind, be his own man instead of the claw of another's hand. He shrugged the thoughts aside. 'I am what I am, and a job is a job,' he told himself. And so he thought of the money instead. But the doubt didn't die easy, and he had to work hard to push it to the back of his mind.

All the while, he was watching the instrument panel. Now he took the control column again. 'Might as well check out Slough terminus en route,' he thought. 'Find out how the institutional lame-brains let this one go.' He liked it when someone took on the establishment. And if it wasn't for people like him, they'd get away with it a lot more often. He overlooked the moral inconsistency. Ethical considerations weren't his strong point. They ended up with him loathing Lawson and loving Lucia. He gave himself over to the way he usually approached his missions. Whether it was him or someone else, they were dead meat now and the flies were buzzing. And it just so happened that he was the fattest.

4

Mark was drowsy. He looked across to Saatchi. She was sleeping. He was tired of looking at nothing through the window and closed his eyes. The dog had put its ugly muzzle down on his feet and slavered over his boot in its sleep. It also came closer to snoring than any animal he had ever heard before. He was decidedly disenchanted with their general situation and his own in particular.

They were waiting, the car dark, still and silent, on the outskirts of the city of Oxford – invisible in the mist and darkness. They had studied the maps, and the place already seemed somehow familiar. On the screen they had a computer-enhanced view of a skyline of spires and domes. But the picture had stayed the same long enough for him to take in every detail several times over, and its novelty value had long since waned. Anyway, he could no longer see it all because Tanya had slumped sideways with her head resting against Paul's shoulder as she slept. His father seemed to be dozing too.

Mark shifted in an attempt to move the dog off his feet, which were going numb, and succeeded only in disturbing Saatchi, who made herself even more comfortable over both sides of the seat. When she settled again, her heel was pressing into the outside of his calf with a painful insistence. He pushed it away, but it was back a few minutes later. Since nobody else would listen, he complained to God in no uncertain terms. A heroic rescue operation shouldn't be like this. That dog, and now his foot, were decidedly smelly. And he realized, with a sinking feeling, that he needed to step outside . . .

With mounting urgency, he counted off the minutes to 4.30 when they had set the alarm to wake them. With the morning light they were counting on Saatchi to recognize the town where she had scavenged for survival all those years ago; and to find in which direction lay Omega 4. Saatchi knew that Omega 4 was somewhere near the city, but it was, after all, an automated prison, and the location was not exactly advertized on cereal packets. As far as the authorities were concerned, there was only one package tour taking in the Omega stations, and only one reason for taking it. Tanya had been unable to find its precise location. But it had to be near where Ghia was taken by the Sentinels. And Saatchi would recognize that place. Her memory held the key. Hence the interdependence between Saatchi's venture and their own.

Taking advantage of her lack of awareness, Mark scrutinized the lines of Saatchi's face, his attention falling at last on the closed eyelids that made her appear completely normal. When she opened her eyes he was doubly startled but did not look away; no need for pretence. She was no stranger to curiosity, and recognized it in his expression. But as she moved her foot away with exaggerated tact, it was clear that she felt no embarrassment. She was stronger than that.

'Sorry about the heel; seems like I made quite an impression while I was asleep.' He was the one who almost blushed, and turned away feeling foolish. He looked out of the window.

The fog must be thinning. There was a single star quite low over the eastern horizon. He watched it idly, and it was some minutes before he realized that it *wasn't*. The motion was almost imperceptible, but it was clearly sinking gradually in the night sky. And stars rise in the east.

He shook the two in the front, and pointed. 'Over there!' and, by way of explanation when they had both found it, 'It's moving in the wrong direction.'

They needed little convincing. Tanya was already bringing the vehicle to life. She was visibly nervous, and it wasn't reassuring to see her so close to fear.

'There's only one thing it could be,' she voiced, leaving the rest to their imaginations, which weren't slow to come up with some frightening speculations. 'The question is: what do we do now?'

'I say we scan,' Paul suggested.

'And advertize our presence?'

'They know that much already,' he came back. 'It's better to know what we're up against.'

The display changed and Tanya examined the picture intently.

'I don't recognize the fingerprint; but it's small and on its own.'

'Which means?'

'Well; given the reluctance of some to venture into these parts . . .' She paused, as if searching for some other conclusion, 'I'd say it was a bounty hunter. Even then, I can only think of two or three who'd tempt fate this far, none of them very pleasant characters.'

She switched back to the view ahead and the car rose, accelerating forwards.

'If anyone has any ideas, I'm open to suggestions.'

'Can we go to ground in the city?'

'I doubt it. I'm not quite sure how they followed us this far, but I am ruling out inspired guesswork. They're trailing us somehow, which means that we can't hide. Also I doubt whether we can run fast enough. Those machines are built for speed – it's a matter of some pride, I might add.'

42

Mark spoke up, 'What are our chances if it comes to a fight?'

Tanya shook her head, 'A, I don't believe in chance; B, it wouldn't be a fight so much as a walkover. We can't match the sort of firepower they'll have on board.'

There was some small interval before Paul ventured, 'That only leaves one option.'

Tanya nodded her assent. 'I was afraid you might disagree.'

'Share it with the rest of us,' said Saatchi, speaking for herself and Mark.

'We need a decoy,' Paul explained. 'It's the car they're following, so we put some buildings between them and us. You three get out and take cover. I draw them away in this,' indicating the vehicle. 'Then somewhere, I suppose, I have to face them. Then if I lose, the three of you still have a way out. You can use the beacon and be picked up in minutes.'

Tanya was negotiating the suburbs of the city. 'You're right about the decoy, Paul, but wrong about the rest.' She paused. 'I think it's fairly clear I should drive the car.' She lifted her voice to override his objections. 'Even if it's just because I know where everything is. Look at the panels – you wouldn't know the half of it . . . and we don't have time right now for me to give you a lesson.' She shrugged. 'Neither do we have time to change places.'

They all recognized a trump card when they saw one. But Paul was struggling with the thought of allowing Tanya to go into that much danger alone. Mark knew that was what was going through his father's head. But he also knew of a way that might resolve the matter quicker than any other – it would help Paul accept her proposal, if Tanya was right.

'I think we should pray,' Mark ventured, 'Individually. And then decide.'

Tanya looked at the screen and judged the distance

separating hunter from hunted. 'We've got a couple of minutes at the most.'

There was quiet. Mark closed his eyes and waited. No time for preamble; he yearned for the presence of God. When he sensed the power in the car he clung to it with his whole being.

'Well?' Tanya's voice broke in.

He opened his eyes and looked across to Saatchi. Her lips were moving soundlessly and then ceased as her eyelids lifted.

'I'm not sure.' Mark struggled. 'I sense reassurance; but it's hard to explain.'

Saatchi was remarkably cool as she spoke into the uncertainty.

'It has to be Tanya.' She turned to Mark and then added firmly, 'I'm quite sure.' She was both sensitive and decisive, maybe they just recognized that; but maybe there was something more that convinced them she was right.

Paul spoke next, reluctantly. 'I think you're right; but I'm not sure why.'

Tanya didn't waste what little time was left by voicing her decision. The screen was alive again as she scanned the city map. Her finger rested on the image.

'This building here; as soon as I can.'

'Got it.' Paul registered.

Saatchi and Mark were scrabbling for kitbags below the seats. The car executed several sharp turns and braked suddenly. They baled out of the back.

Paul hesitated and found Tanya looking at him. And he felt humbled by the courage in her eyes.

'Help me, Paul: don't stop praying.' The words blurted out through a chink in the contained emotion. She turned away. 'Find Natasha. I love you two more than anyone else. So go on.'

He moved and the car was empty. Then it was

moving again, and picking up speed, Tanya's hands and feet on the controls. She examined her knuckles whitening on the steering wheel and whispered, 'Well, Lord: here I am.' Then she wiped her hand irritably over both eyes as her vision began to swim. This certainly was not the time to cry. She bit her lip and lashed out against the fear settling on the car. And in the heart of darkness reaching out to take her, there was a moment's recoil, and surprise at the faith that could somehow make her feel even now that the victory would be hers.

Mark and Saatchi gained the safety of the shadows. When they turned, Paul had just emerged from the car. Even as it started to move, they caught the faint sound of engines in the direction they had just come from. Paul was standing motionless in the road. It seemed unreal. Mark shouted across the few yards between them. He tried to go back out and pull him in, but did not dare. By now the noise was too loud. Saatchi cried out sharply.

Paul was beyond hearing. Tanya didn't expect to see him again. He knew that. Otherwise she would never have said that. The night air was cold, damp and unpleasantly scented. The sensations somehow crystallized. Suddenly it was very quiet.

Mark turned and saw a search beam travelling along the street with agonizing certainty to where his father was standing. He tried to close his eyes and couldn't.

Paul came to life, half-turned and continued the movement as the spotlight reached him to roll sideways out of its glare. The beam swept over the empty space where he had been standing a moment before. He reached the arched entrance where the others were crouching, and flattened himself against the stone wall.

The pursuit machine flashed by, a blur of searchlights and hideous bulk; the sound of its engines a doppler howl in their ears. Paul stared after the vanishing form.

Mark's touch on his shoulder made him turn.

'Should we go now, or wait?'

Saatchi was standing a little to one side watching him intently. Paul looked from one to the other, tried to clear his mind and make the right decision. He thought for a moment back along the route they had taken to this place and searched the silhouetted spires for the answer to their location. Three landmarks recognized, and he knew where they were.

He looked along the street to the opening at the far end, and the corner at which Tanya had turned left. They would go right. About a hundred yards along, on the far side, was the building she had indicated as the rendezvous.

They were still waiting.

'We'd better go now.' Already the two vehicles had been swallowed up by the night; there was no sight or sound of them. The mist was thinning, they could see a good distance in any direction. All the time, his thoughts were with Tanya in silent prayer.

'Ready?'

They nodded. Saatchi called softly and the dog reappeared at her side, slipping out of the shadow of the cloisters. They moved out along the street.

When the flash came, they were out in the open. It was a flicker so brief it could almost have been imagined. But it was followed a moment later by a crackling report and something like a badly timed drumroll. Eyes and ears strained for something else, but the ensuing silence was relentless.

Saatchi was the first to break free and run the short distance to cover, followed by Mark and lastly Paul. Dimly it registered that they were in the right place. The door was jammed and they entered by a broken bay

46

window, then moved back through the building, using pencil-beam torches to inspect.

The interior was largely free of damage. Books lined the shelves, unread, neatly arrayed, some permanently 'Reduced' in the last few days of a sale more than twelve years before. But the prices now were as meaningless as the endless shelves of forgotten lore.

Paul was the first to hear the sound of an engine; and the first to get back to the windows and see the small bright dot — search beams playing over the buildings — hanging over the city perhaps half a mile away. The significance of that speck burned itself into his mind like focussed sunlight on tissue paper. It held his eyes, and he found himself willing it to fall from the sky with a vehemence he seemed powerless to prevent. And as he fought the desire for vengeance, it seemed to him that the Lord who was his helper was a million miles away and looking in the opposite direction.

Saatchi was on the floor, sitting with her back against the wall, her legs stretched out and her feet against the facing bookshelf. The dog lay by her, its head in her lap, looking up at her mournfully. She was speaking the language of her childhood softly into the silence, and the animal's ears moved from time to time as it recognized familiar phrases. Her right arm lay across the dog's shoulders and the fingers of her hand moved gently over its head as it nuzzled against her.

Her other hand lay open palm upwards beside her thigh.

She had long since abandoned the fruitless churning of muddled thoughts and was communing freely with her God, finding peace that persisted in the bleakness of their situation.

Mark was stretched out horizontally, almost sleeping. From time to time he opened his eyes to look at the ceiling. The regimented rows of high shelving on either side enclosed the area in which he and Saatchi were lying. But the perspective played tricks in this dim light and, tired as he was, it looked for all the world as if the walls of books were tilting inwards, ready to fall from the shelves and bury them. Although it was only an illusion, he couldn't quite feel easy as he lay there. And it was just one more thing to keep him from sleeping.

All the time he was half listening to the sound of Saatchi's voice. The rest of his mind dwelt on Tanya, and tried to reconcile events with the feeling of reassurance he had known earlier. A spoken word broke into his thoughts.

'Mark?'

'Mmm?'

'Are you trying to sleep?'

'Not really.'

'Thinking about Tanya?'

'When I'm not trying not to,' he replied, and then, 'Yes, I suppose so.' Silence for a while, and then,

'Mark?'

'Yes?'

A pause.

'There's something I'd like to tell you.'

'Is it good news?'

'Yes.'

'Good.' He began to have the feeling this

conversation was leading somewhere. He waited for it to get to wherever it was going, and finally it did.

'I think we're going to find them.'

He opened his eyes and looked across at her for some time before closing them again and turning his face back toward the ceiling.

'So do I.'

Her next statement was unexpected.

'I'm afraid,' she admitted.

'Me too.'

She looked across to the makeshift barricade about fifteen feet away that they had placed as a screen between themselves and the front of the building. Paul was crouching behind it, watching, still, his back turned to them.

'I'm not sure your father can cope,' said Saatchi quietly.

'Oh? What makes you say that?'

'Mmm,' she pondered, 'It's something to do with your mother and Tanya. Maybe because they're twins. If Tanya's . . .' she paused, '*dead* . . .', saying the word as if she didn't want it to touch her mouth on its way out, 'I don't know what it will do to him. They must be so similar. It would be like losing Natasha twice.'

He could see what she meant, and imagined his father to be under more pressure at that moment than at any other since the time, eleven years before, when he had had to escape with Mark and leave Natasha behind. But God had brought them this far.

'He'll come through,' Mark assured her, and himself as well. 'It's going to be all right. He'll know what to do.'

There were no further exchanges and they settled back into their own thoughts. Phoenix stirred and lifted her head. Then she sat up, looking over in Paul's direction. Finally, she walked slowly over to where he crouched, and stood beside him.

Paul became aware of the animal by his side, but continued staring straight ahead. He was watching something; or thought he was, and the dog's attitude leant weight to his suspicion. There was a low growl in its throat. Its attention was on the same small group of shadows as his own. He became horribly certain that the composition of that cluster of forms was changing; that it wasn't the dim light, or lack of sleep, but that something was there. And the smell of this thing was different from what he had smelt before. Different because it was like nothing he had ever smelt before; and different because the dog could smell it too.

Now faint sounds carried to him; shuffling, searching sounds. Then he distinctly heard the clear slap of a book falling to the floor. Almost immediately Saatchi was by his side, her body tense, eyes straining forward into the gloom. As she watched, her lips moved and whispered a word into the stillness. She was as frightened as a child alone in the dark.

Paul wrestled with the thought that in this place of death there was something alive and – much worse – that 'it' had come looking for them.

The tension snapped as the dog bounded forwards, scattering the crude barricade with its forelegs. There was a cry from Saatchi and she leapt after it, then fell in a confused heap amongst the debris with Paul pinning her to the floor. She struggled and tried to kick free. He wasn't about to lose a second member of their party to whatever was out there, and he held her captive. They both heard the snarl and the sudden blow that ended it, followed by several indistinct noises as of something moving awkwardly near the front of the building. The noises went. And Phoenix had gone.

Paul released Saatchi and she scrambled forwards, stumbling heavily against some unseen obstacle. But she hardly noticed the pain in her shin. Only one thing concerned her – what had happened to her dog?

She made her way to the front of the building where the animal had disappeared. The others stood watching her torchlight ranging over the area inside the window bay as she moved around.

Eventually Mark went over to her. She was kneeling examining a small patch of floorspace, and he squatted beside her to see what she had found. He did not need to look very hard to know that it was blood. It was sticky to the touch, and stained his finger red in the torchlight.

'That's all?' he asked, in disbelief at the dog's sudden disappearance.

'There's some more over there,' she motioned towards the window. 'Just one or two splashes. And some dirt streaks that might have been there for years. That's just about it. I'm not about to follow it outside until there's some light.'

'I don't know what to say,' he said, switching off his torch. 'I just don't understand what's going on any more. What on earth was that, and what was it doing here?'

'Looking for us,' she said coldly. 'Instead it found Phoenix.' She was struggling against tears. 'If it wasn't for Ghia I'd think it was the biggest mistake I ever made coming back here. But I'll find him.'

Mark wanted to help her. He reached out and took her hand. He wiped the bloodstains from her fingers. She was shaking with emotion and cried briefly.

'We'll find him,' he reassured her. 'And maybe Phoenix too.'

'I could have stopped it,' she said quietly.

'Maybe: maybe not. Dad was only trying to protect you,' he ventured.

'I know,' she admitted. 'I'm sure he did what he thought best.' Her voice dropped. 'It's just that Phoenix is gone now, and I might have been able to stop it.'

They stood up and she switched off her torch and turned away from him to look out of the window for some minutes.

'It's starting to get light,' she said in a voice somehow flat and empty. Then she turned back and regarded him frankly.

'Mark, I just don't know how God's going to get us out of this one.'

//

A dull grey morning was slowly emerging from the night mists, and the company of three prepared to face it, disconsolate and uncomfortable. Clothes worn overnight retained the sweat and dirt of the day before, smelling faintly. Breath was stale, skin greasy and eyes itching. They ate without enthusiasm or conversation.

Eventually Paul broached the day's business.

'We need some answers,' he said gently. 'First: we need to know exactly what happened to Tanya. She may be alive; injured or captured. So I want to take a look at the wreck. Depending on what I find, we can plan accordingly.' The others nodded their agreement and he continued.

'Second: we've got to find out whether Saatchi can remember enough to recognize the way to the Omega camp. The nearest vantage point is the cupola of the building directly opposite. We can go over there together and I can leave you inside to get your bearings while I go off on my own. The kit had better stay with you.' He paused. 'Any questions about that?'

Saatchi looked up. 'How long do we wait?'

'Give me an hour,' Paul replied. 'If I run into our friend—' He paused, 'it may take me a while to deal with him. But I'll be back.'

She looked across at Mark. 'An hour's fine by me. Mark?'

He nodded assent. 'I'm not happy about splitting up,' he said.

'I understand how you feel,' said Paul. 'But I think we'll get things done quicker that way. After last night, I don't want to stay here any longer than necessary. Which brings me to another point. You said something last night, Saatchi. It was just a word. I wondered what it meant.'

She flushed and translated. 'It means "dark ones". I don't know,' she shrugged. 'I stopped believing in them a long time ago. When I was here before, as a child, it was a name I had for things that went bump in the night. You've got to remember there were just the two of us, Ghia and me, and we were scared most of the time, particularly at night. I suppose it helped to have a name to cut the terror down to size.'

'Maybe you did imagine it,' Mark offered. 'But maybe there really was something. Something you heard or caught glimpses of. It's possible.'

'I suppose so. We were alive after the fighting, and I know other things were too – for a while. But they weren't threatening and didn't last long themselves. Phoenix hunted some of them; the ones that weren't diseased. She wouldn't eat the meat once they'd started to go, I remember that.'

'I don't quite understand what went on here,' Mark said. 'From the buildings, you'd think nothing much; nothing nuclear for certain. But it seems totally dead; a real ghost town. It doesn't make sense.'

'I don't know much more myself,' Saatchi admitted. 'As far as radiation goes, I don't think it was so much a direct hit as strikes against bases nearby. We're ringed by seven or eight targets here, or were. I think what took the population out was something else. The really dirty stuff was biochemical; short-life pathogens, other things there aren't any names for. I think that's what happened here.'

'So how come you and your brother survived?' Mark queried.

She shrugged. 'Who knows? Maybe we were born just after it happened. Maybe we had a mother, or friends, who lived long enough to keep us alive until Ghia was taken by the Sentinels. Maybe those friends were the ones who got me to safety forty miles away. Maybe this . . .' She lifted her chin and reached inside her jacket top to lift out a small polished stone threaded on a silver chain, 'belonged to one of them. Apparently it was tied round my neck with string when they found me. As I said: who knows?'

Paul took up the conversation. 'Well, if it was something like that, and the time scale went wrong somehow so that things were still dying months or years later, that would explain why the Empire stays well clear. It also means we could be running more risk than I imagined.'

Mark snorted in disgust. 'What the Empire did to this place really stinks,' he said.

Saatchi looked at Paul quizzically. 'Did you notice anything else last night; besides the noises?'

He knew what she meant immediately. 'The smell.'

She nodded agreement. 'That was the way the dead meat used to smell. And sometimes, when we cooked it, something that looked all right used to be the same. We never ate that stuff.' She voiced the obvious conclusion for them all. 'Whatever was here last night still had the disease.'

Paul muttered something under his breath then said with urgency, 'Look: we've got to move quickly. I don't want to be stuck here through another night.'

He paused and rubbed his eyes wearily before continuing.

'On the other hand, I don't want to go out there or do anything until we've talked something through. What happened last night was understandable, but I think we can do better.'

He avoided looking directly at either of them as he went on. 'I just want you two to realize that I'm responsible for you both. And if you don't let me do the job properly, we're going to bring the whole thing down around our ears. I must be able to rely on you,' he concluded. 'And you have to trust my judgment.'

His words sank in during the silence that followed. Once he felt the point had been taken, he continued.

'There's a lot of opposition to our being here and what we're trying to do. My guess is you felt as oppressed as I did last night. And I think we've given enough ground, don't you? It's time we took some back.'

It was an immense effort for Saatchi to look him in the eye.

'Sure. You're right,' she affirmed. 'We aren't getting anywhere like this.'

They began to pray, faltering and uncertain, and once again began to draw together. And as they prayed, declaring the lordship of Christ, they felt their spirits rise and sensed again the promise of victory. When they rose to leave it seemed that they had begun to break through.

Devo leaned back in the padded leather seat and took stock. There had been only one person in the car; he was fairly sure of that. So the other three were still around somewhere – that's if Slough terminus were seeing straight. He only had their word that there were four people. But a hunch said they were right. So he'd fouled up, but it could have been worse. The others would show eventually if he hung round long enough; they had to. Sooner or later they would move on foot out into the open.

Two things bothered him. First: after a chase in which he'd gained little ground at all, because of the skill of the other driver, he was surprised at such an unforced error creeping in. Second: despite the fact that it was a total write-off, he'd have expected to find something in the wreckage, no matter how charred. Either the body had been flung well clear – and he had looked pretty hard – or else there had been no mistake at all and there were still four people out there. In which case, where and when had driver and vehicle parted company?

Whichever way you looked at it, he noted with satisfaction, there were still pickings to be had. He leaned forward, flipped a switch, and the hatch opened on hydraulics. He took a look outside. Uninviting. But experience told him a short reconnaissance might pay dividends.

Mark and Saatchi were leaning forward against the solid wooden window sill, staring out through the windows of the cupola. It was a view that, in its time, had been enjoyed by many a tourist for the breathtaking proximity of the surrounding rooftops, and the grandeur of the architecture rising on all sides. But their purpose was more serious. The panes of glass, surprisingly intact, afforded a protected outlook over the streets of the city, and it was this that they hoped to use to their advantage.

Mark turned from a leisurely wondering over a bridge that seemed oddly out of place, spanning hardly anything at all, to see how Saatchi was getting on in making sense of their surroundings.

She glanced across at him, and her expression was serious.

'It's no good,' she said. 'I can't remember. They all look the same.'

He crossed the bare wooden floor and looked out of the opposite window. It was true. In any direction there stretched a vista of jumbled spires and towers. Each one was special enough to be a landmark, but put them all together and . . . He shook his head; it was too chaotic. And it made him realize she might not be able to point out the direction of the Omega camp.

He crossed over to her. 'It's not your fault,' he reassured her. 'It was a lot to expect.'

She gave him a desolate look. 'I never thought I'd forget. In all these years it never entered my head.' Her hopelessness was painful.

'It all looks familiar; but I can't seem to use it to work out which direction we need to be going. And another thing,' she added, in a tone that seemed to imply that it was particularly significant, 'I know it might seem strange,' she hedged, 'with all these spires and things everywhere, but the one I remember most of all I can't see. These are all too beautiful; it was really quite plain – sort of fat.'

Mark felt bewildered. He had never seen so many

shapes and sizes. There were dozens of them; it wasn't as if there was a shortage to choose from. He was inclined to doubt her. She could be just failing to recognize the critical one among all the others. Maybe she needed to relax for a while and pray; let all the new images sink in and wait for the right one to come to the surface.

'There's still time,' he tried to encourage her. 'It might come back.'

She looked away to the north. 'Maybe. Ghia's out there somewhere. I've got to remember.' She turned to leave, still deep in thought, searching the recesses of her mind.

Mark stayed behind for some minutes after she descended the few steps to the roof space below and then the several wooden flights down to floor level, listening to the receding sound of her footsteps, and then standing quietly, gazing into the distance.

The camp was nearby. And the camp held his mother and Saatchi's brother. It *couldn't* be right if they didn't find them now, and if Tanya wasn't still alive somewhere. He knew enough to recognize the Lord's touch on their circumstances and to know that events didn't miss the mark by that far. He was expecting something much closer to success before he would be satisfied that God had had his last word on the matter. He followed Saatchi downstairs.

He was surprised to find the theatre empty and the heavy wooden door ajar. He crossed the floor quickly and went outside. Saatchi was crouching in the road and he guessed immediately that she was following the blood trail from the shop front. She was working her way slowly towards the part of the road that showed signs of subsidence. The road's surface there had fractured and formed a gentle concavity around a small bomb crater. It was one of the few visible signs of structural damage they had seen.

Something put him on edge. She was totally absorbed and at the same time exposed. He checked in all directions before crossing the open space to join her.

'You've got a nerve,' he whispered as he reached her. 'You could get us both killed.'

'I had to find out,' she said. 'It won't take long. Look.'

She was right; the trail was easy to follow. It led to the centre of the bomb damage where whole slabs of road-metal had heaved upwards and lay haphazardly tilted skywards. He was reminded of skating on thin ice as he cast a wary eye over the crazy paving across which the red splashes led.

'You're not thinking of going across that . . .' he said, knowing full well she was.

'What do you think?' she said.

'Please,' he urged.

'Look,' she said, with something approaching impatience. 'Something else clearly went that way; I'm willing to risk it.'

Mark could no longer ignore the rising emotion telling him they should not be there. Somehow he had to get Saatchi back under cover. But he was denied the time to try and convince her.

'Don't move!'

A shout echoed off the buildings. Twenty yards away, sheltered in a doorway, stood a figure watching them through a set of gunsights, the weapon levelled in their direction.

They stopped, freeze-frame, in mid-gesture. Something like lead settled in Mark's stomach. They had been warned, and he'd missed it. From the moment he had seen Saatchi crouching in the street a voice had been telling him with quiet insistence to go and get her. He should have known what was happening.

'*It's too late now,*' the suggestion came to him. '*You've blown it.*' And try as he might to stand against it, the insistence that they were both condemned because of their failure to obey was an iron hand tightening on his throat with a vice-like grip.

'Stand up straight. Hands on your head. Now turn around.'

They complied and stood waiting side by side until the voice came again, nearer this time and directly behind them.

'Where are the others?'

'There aren't any others,' Saatchi replied, risking the obvious lie. 'There were three of us. You know what happened to the other.'

These words seemed to be weighed. Then she uttered a half cry as the weapon fired, placing a shot directly between them about a metre ahead on the road. There was a pause for emphasis.

'The lady with the mouth: move away two steps to the left.'

Mark watched the gap between them widen.

'You: three paces forward; where she can see you.'

Mark's mind blanked. Time seemed to slow right down. He took a step forward, then another. And finally the last footfall. He rocked on his feet.

'*Lord, stop this.*' The words were unvoiced but seemed without life. '*It can't happen.*' A wall of darkness had completely enclosed him. He spoke to it. '*It can't happen.*'

'Now, I don't suppose any of us believes for one moment that I'm about to teach a new dance routine here . . .' came the voice. 'So let's do it once more. Where are the others?'

Mark swayed slightly, leg muscles shaking. Thought ground to a halt. And then the lengthening silence was filled with sound. He heard the beginning of a cry that seemed to come from afar, but in reality came from him, and then darkness enveloped him and he plunged into the abyss.

Paul started at the sound of the shot. He knew instinctively that it came from the direction in which he had left the others. He cast a last look over the wreckage, turned and ran back the way he had come, drawing the baraq and shield from his belt as he ran.

At the corner, he took in the situation at a glance. Saatchi was standing with her back to him in the centre of the street. Just behind her was the bounty hunter. There was no sign of Mark. He approached cautiously, using the buildings for cover. He was perhaps thirty yards away when the other turned, and though he ducked quickly, it was obvious he had been seen. He let the weapons drop casually the few inches to the ground and stood up straight, rolling them into the shadows with his foot at the same time.

The mercenary was leaving him in no doubt as to what would happen to Saatchi should he make a suspicious move; the muzzle of the weapon was barely inches away from her spine. He moved forwards carefully as ordered, all the while searching for some sign of Mark.

'Over there,' the other pointed crudely. 'Get him out.'

When he looked in the direction indicated, there seemed to be little except a heap of rubble. But, moving forwards, he saw the cavity, framed by jagged chunks of tarmac and concrete.

'Mark?' he called down into the darkness.

'Dad.'

It was a voice from the pit, shaky but with a hopeful edge.

Standing at the very lip of the crater, Mark had been pitched forwards into the darkness as the fractured concrete moved under his weight. He was surprised to be alive. As for the bounty hunter; it didn't matter either way. All he had been waiting for was for Paul to appear. Now he had them all.

'Mark. How deep are you?'

'Not very. Twelve feet maybe. I'm on a pile of rubble. It seems to go most of the way to the surface.'

Paul's eyes were adjusting to the gloom. 'I can see it. I'm climbing down.' He turned to the others.

Devo shrugged. 'Go ahead. Just don't keep me waiting too long.' He completed the threat by a gesture of the weapon at Saatchi's back.

Paul negotiated the entrance to the shaft and dropped out of sight. The man with the gun cast an appreciative eye over his hostage.

'Too bad you got mixed up with these punks,' he offered conversationally.

'I'm looking for my brother,' she replied simply.

'In this dump?' He took in their surroundings. 'Sounds like a long shot to me.'

She ignored his appraisal. 'Who do you work for?'

'Who does everybody work for?'

She caught the disdain in his voice. 'You're going to take us back,' she said.

'Right first time.'

'How much are we worth?'

'Probably not as much as you'd like to think,' he countered.

'Can I turn round?' she asked.

He backed off a couple of paces. 'I'd appreciate the change of view.'

She turned slowly. Every nerve sent the message that she was taking a risk, but there was nothing to lose. She stared him out.

'Do you think I'm worth more?'

He bounced the question around in his head a few times, looking at it from all angles and twisting its meaning. He clearly enjoyed making the valuation. Then eventually came up with a judgment.

'I'd say you were worth a lot more.' He paused. 'I like a woman who doesn't give up,' he complimented, 'even if she does lack a certain subtlety.'

She flushed. 'Look. We're just ordinary people. We aren't criminals. Why don't you just leave us alone? Pretend you never saw us? You don't have to take us back.' She realized she was talking to someone with a lifetime's killing behind him. But nobody *wanted* that sort of existence, did they?

From his expression, it didn't seem as if she was making much of an impression. But she couldn't afford to give up trying.

'It can't be easy – working for them,' she said. 'We both know what they are. At least you've got guts. And I'd say you were worth a lot more – than they pay.' She successfully turned the judgment round.

He watched her closely. 'You certainly have a strong line in hard talking.' He thought it over and her hopes began to rise; but then he half-smiled. 'Too bad I'm just a businessman at heart.'

Mark was lying on a sloping floor some fifteen feet below the surface. The tunnel led away into the darkness in both directions. Behind and supporting him was a framed mesh cage running the length of the passage and containing what he dimly perceived to be a mechanical conveyor system. A bundle of piped conduits ran overhead—arteries in the concrete construction of which the tunnel formed a limb.

He was still trembling, although the ground was now steady. His hurts from the fall were minor. As the surface at the lip of the crater had given way under his weight, his legs had buckled as in a faint, and he had slid down the heap of crumbled masonry feet first, escaping a knock to the head.

Paul helped him up, and they rested for a few moments against the grille, taking air in short, shallow breaths while waiting to regain strength. There was an overpowering stench. They could taste it on the backs of their tongues. They watched nervously in both directions for signs of life, but in the near darkness, they could have been approached to less than ten feet away and not know it.

They turned at last and scrambled back to the surface, Mark emerging first with Paul providing support from below. Above ground, nothing had changed. Saatchi was still covered by the mercenary's gun. He stuffed a lighter into his jacket pocket as they brushed themselves free of some of the dirt in the tunnel, and drew contentedly on the fresh cigar. No reason not to mix business with pleasure. Eventually he was ready.

'Okay: you'll do,' he commented. 'You're travelling second class anyhow, and I don't mind a bit of dirt. Move over here. Unless you have any objections I think we'll be on our way.'

14

The cell built into the rear of the vehicle was windowless and without illumination. Neither was there any obvious source of fresh air.

'You two stink.'

Saatchi voiced her disgust at the two bodies pressed against her on either side. The smell in the tunnel had attached itself to them.

'You're not exactly a fragrant offering yourself,' Mark replied. The air in the confined space was quite foul.

They waited in silence for something to happen. Eventually Paul inquired casually, 'I don't suppose either of you has the impression we're actually moving?'

'No,' they responded in unison.

'In that case,' – he thought a little further – 'what's going on? Our man doesn't seem the sort to waste time. So what's taking so long?'

They pondered a while. Then Paul continued, 'I think it's time to exercise a little faith.' He paused. 'I'd say something's gone wrong. And if prayer can move mountains, it's time we made it even more wrong.'

Again they started, belatedly, to stir their spirits and bring an extra dimension to bear on the forces that held them captive. But though they had been tardy, another had not. The wheels of power, whose momentum they now caught, had been turning, unnoticed, events in their favour.

Paul remembered he had not told them what he had uncovered. 'I've seen the wreckage,' he said. 'And there was no sign of Tanya: nothing at all. I don't know how, but I think she survived. Maybe she's got something to do with whatever's going on out there.'

Saatchi thought otherwise. 'I'd like to think so,' she began, 'but I think it's something else. I can't quite make it out, but I think there's someone or something involved here that we don't even know about; something that we just aren't taking into account. I can't get any further than that,' she admitted.

Without warning, the rear door opened. They blinked in the sudden light. Devo ordered them out and lined them up against a wall. He studied the ground at his feet a while then looked up at them.

'Seems like your friend had a busy morning,' he said. He scrutinized their expressions, then addressed Paul. 'Or maybe it was you.' He pointed the gun at Mark at about stomach level. 'So why don't you tell me where you were earlier this morning?'

'I was at the wreck,' Paul volunteered quickly. The gun remained levelled.

'And what did you see?'

'The car was burnt out. There was no sign of Tanya in the wreckage.'

Devo's eyebrows lifted. 'I see; a woman driver.' He paused. 'Wife? No, I don't think so. Lover then.' He smiled sardonically at Paul's response, 'I see you prefer the term "friend"; or "colleague" perhaps.' The barrel of the gun lifted. 'At least you had the sense not to lie.'

He tilted his head and watched them sideways, the muscles of his face set in a hard frown. 'So. Here we are – and here we stay. Until your friend, wherever she is, makes her move.' He cast his eyes briefly to the skyline. 'And when she does, I'll be ready for her.'

15

By some strange coincidence they were again returned to the curiously-shaped building they had explored before. The structure, designed like a classical amphitheatre, had appealed to Devo's grim humour as the stage for a drama that was to be both brief and conclusive.

It was dusk. Inside the building, the light was failing steadily. Paul, Mark and Saatchi were lying, handcuffed, sweat-streaked and tired, at the edge of the circular floorspace beneath the ornate ceiling of the Sheldonian theatre. Gradually, the winged cherubs toiling overhead withdrew into the invisible heavens, as if shy of witnessing the night's events; the canopy of darkness shrouding the canopy of paint. Colours faded into greyness and, eventually, darkness.

Mark's eye settled on the silhouette of a hatchet and sticks jutting horizontally from the wall over the door to his right, symbols of the power of an empire long gone. In reality, the same threat hung over themselves and Tanya. He wondered exactly what the mercenary had prepared for her if indeed she tried to liberate them during the hours of darkness. The thought of having to watch as she walked into a trap was torture, but with their hands bound it seemed there was little they could do.

The temperature was dropping uncomfortably low and Mark shuffled closer against Saatchi for warmth and company. She half opened her eyes and acknowledged him with a tired smile.

'What's he doing now?'

'Still checking,' came the reply. 'Somewhere over by the lights.'

'Do you think she'll come?'

'I hope not.' He raised himself on one elbow from where he could see the twin spotlights either side of the entrance and the figure crouched between them, checking the cables.

He grunted. 'Ever prayed for equipment failure?' he asked half jokingly.

She managed a smile; the thought appealed. 'Can't say I have.'

'Wouldn't do any harm,' he commented wryly. 'It's bad enough that Tanya might walk right into all this, but I hate to think how your "dark ones" would react to finding themselves centre-stage.

'Don't even think about it,' she advised, lifting her handcuffed wrists. 'Trussed up in these, I feel like the first course.' They heard footsteps approaching and fell silent.

'I see you made yourselves cosy. Just thought I'd let you know everything's ready.' Devo surveyed the set-up: barrier, lights and power pack, infra-red trap across the door and manual over-ride. Armoury right by his side. He seated himself on the second tier of the sloping bench-clad platform bordering the central stage of the room, and bit off the end of a cigar. The lighter flared briefly, and then the glowing end was all that remained to betray his presence in the darkness. Made him a bit of a target, he knew; but anything coming through that door was going to be so blinded it hardly mattered. Anyway, he sensed, he had a while yet. He looked down at the three huddled on the floor in the small space defined by the barricade and felt slightly envious. It was getting cold. He drew his flak jacket closer and tried to concentrate on the cigar.

16

There was a sudden draught in the room, and Devo's mind snapped to the alert. The young woman sleeping soundly on the floor had triggered thoughts of Lucia and he had been drifting in reminiscence. The hostages had not moved, but he was aware that something had changed and brought him out of his reverie. Draughts meant open doors, and he strained to catch any sound in that direction. His mind went to the trap he had set, willing the equipment not to let him down. A glance at his watch: 2.25 a.m.

He rose and moved away soundlessly from where he had been sitting. A couple of feet away lay the security of his arms cache. His fingers closed around a weapon and lifted it soundlessly from the table.

Something skittered across the floor to his right, in the direction he had come from. He fired twice at the sound in automatic response, the gun flashing in the dark. He hit the lights button. Nothing happened.

'So much for being clever,' he told himself and was suddenly afraid. There was another sound, high up on his left. Something snaked across towards him through the air in a long arc that ended at the barrel of his gun. He felt something light fall across his wrists, and in the same instant a touch on his left shoulder. A second too late he recognized the feel of rope on the skin of his neck and wrists. There was a sharp burning as the nooses tightened. Then he was yanked rudely from his feet and smashed into and through the barricade. The last thing he knew was the explosion of pain in his head as he hit the floor.

Mark, Paul and Saatchi witnessed the several stages of abduction through rising levels of consciousness. Two things bore in upon them: the realization that something was in the room, and the knowledge that their chained wrists meant they were helpless to protect themselves. They made no sound in the hope that this would avoid attracting attention in their direction. Not that this meant there was silence. There were plenty of sounds being made elsewhere in the room, and these were startlingly similar to those of the previous night accompanying the sudden disappearance of Phoenix.

True to form, the commotion ceased as enigmatically as it had begun. Nothing seemed to have changed, except that now there were just the three of them. Paul jack-knifed into a sitting position and peered over the protective wall behind which they had been so effectively hidden. The room was, apart from themselves, quite empty.

There was some wriggling from the other two.

'I don't suppose he dropped his keys?' enquired Saatchi, feeling it was unnecessary to preface this by any of the obvious statements she could have made in the circumstances, such as 'What happened?'

'I doubt it,' Paul replied 'When it's that convenient it only happens in films. But we'll take a look after.'

'So,' and this time it was obvious, 'What now?'

Paul shrugged. 'Well, I can't say I'm that sad to see the back of him. And I don't feel particularly like forming a search party as a result. I'd say there's absolutely nothing we can do. So we might as well stay here and keep out of trouble.'

'I suppose they could have taken us too if they'd wanted,' Mark commented.

'Exactly. And if we go poking our noses around outside they may decide to do just that.'

'You seem pretty convinced we're dealing with people,' Saatchi observed.

'They took him at a distance,' Paul explained, 'which is all you can do when you're facing a gun. I expect they used ropes. All in all, much too much method for a wild animal. I'd say your 'dark ones' are human all right. In fact, I'd call them survivors. But how is anybody's guess.'

He paused and then added quietly; 'I know where, though.' And so did they all. The underground chasm, dark as death, had claimed another victim.

17

Paul stood looking across the street at the dark unknown which lay in wait for them all. The Empire had been ruthless in combating the disease that had been unleashed upon the city. All survivors had been killed, their bodies burned. But they had not been careful enough. When the exterminators left, the rot had remained behind, smelling faintly and working its way underground. If the three of them were to find Tanya and Phoenix, they were going to have to follow it down.

Paul gave the crater a wide berth as he made his way back along the street to the point where he had dropped the baraq and shield. They lay there still, and he stopped to retrieve them into manacled hands.

With these two weapons he could face any foe. The baraq of a Knight of the Church held a power far beyond that of any ordinary weapon. The princples of its engineering had enabled the Church to harness one of the fundamental forces of the universe. A parallel application had produced the shield which rendered their spacecraft inviolable to the Empire's arsenal, and which in a more modest form would protect Paul now.

He shuddered to think that the scientists on Ekklesia had for the purpose of this mission given him the means to amplify the baraq's power still further. Despite what he knew of them, the Sentinels held little fear for a man armed with such a weapon.

Returning the way he had come, Paul entered again the building where the others were sitting, waiting.

Light was slanting in through a high east window, falling upon the youthful forms prone upon the floor, and illuminating the scene. Searching out line of temple, eyelid closed, cheek smooth, mouth slack and weary. Clothing crumpled and shabby. Hands together, but not from choice. A renaissance painting came to mind, set against the contemporary image. There the figure kneeling in acceptance, turned to face the quickening ray and receive the message of hope. Here the weary human frame struck sideways a glancing blow and on the beam a different meaning. Unfathomable. He felt a weariness for the day. Not only for himself; but because there was nothing better for its light to fall upon. Looking at them, knowing how they felt, filled him with remorse. And inside him, half unvoiced, was the question that had echoed down the ages. *'How long, Lord? How long?'*

His footsteps sounded softly and their eyes opened.

'At least we can be rid of these,' he offered, indicating both handcuffs and the means of their removal with a single gesture.

They got to their feet and followed him over to the table. Pulling up a chair, he sat down.

'Mark first.'

His son placed both hands, knuckles outwards, fingers curled under, firmly on the wooden surface, wrists as parted as allowed, exposing the mechanism of the handcuffs a slender air-gap away from the inner surface of his wrist.

His father held with two-handed grip the baraq vertical, or nearly so, and pressed against Mark's inner forearm. There was a moment's deliberation, then a searing flash and the hand was free. The acrid smell of burning wood and a wisp of smoke rose from a black-rimmed hole beneath the beam. The metal jaws clattered onto the table top and were swept aside. This process repeated, his other wrist was freed. And then those of the girl. Which brought them inevitably to the next problem – the prisoner cannot free himself.

Mark and Paul exchanged looks.

'You know I can't do it,' Paul said. He offered the cylinder across the table.

'I know.'

The baraq changed hands and they changed places.

Paul laid his forearms down on the table. 'You only have to break the centre link,' he reassured Mark, 'I can live with them round my wrists for the time being as long as my hands are free.'

Mark adjusted his grip on the weapon and positioned it over and between his father's wrists.

'Okay: I've got it.' He squeezed gently and frowned when nothing happened.

'Wrong pressure pattern,' Paul explained. 'Try again over there.'

This time, some distance across the wooden surface,

the baraq discharged a bolt of energy against the table top.

'The action's slightly firmer than the ones we train with,' Mark explained. 'I've got it now.'

Again the flash, and the metal parted. Paul took back the cylinder.

'Two of the kitbags have gone,' Saatchi observed. 'There's plenty of food and drink, but that's about all.'

'I spotted that already,' said Paul. 'We'd better eat. Give us time to think things through a bit. Though I think our next move is fairly clear.'

In the end, they drank more than they ate. It seemed to help. Discussion was brief. If they turned back there was a long trek back to civilization and the likelihood of being picked up by Security patrols. They couldn't get away, because the beacon with which to summon the ship to lift them out was in one of the missing kitbags. And they couldn't stay put indefinitely. The only way left to go was after the others.

Phoenix had been taken into the underground passages – the blood trail made that clear. And Paul was quite certain now that the reason Tanya had disappeared was not that she had perished in the crash, but that she had survived and been taken to the same place. It was time to confront the Dark Ones, whoever or whatever they were.

They were standing in the tunnel directly beneath the entrance, at the base of the rubble heap which had broken Mark's fall earlier. From the baraq in Paul's right hand a diffuse light reached into the gloom, to which their eyes were gradually adapting. Mark shifted the weight of the power pack slung across his shoulder and peered down, checking the terminal connections more by feel than anything else. They seemed good.

The pack was against his left hip. One hand fingered the dial nervously, ready to turn up the voltage. The other held one of the two spotlights that had failed to work the night before. A longer cable draped away to the second spot held by Saatchi. The leads, parted earlier, were newly spliced. She also held a small gun taken from the arsenal of their captor. But she had to admit all it made her feel was uncomfortable.

As he looked squarely into the darkness and felt the floor of the tunnel sloping down under them, Mark could not help thinking of the image of *Sheol*, the unfathomable depths where the lost souls roamed. He shivered suddenly. David, the warrior-king, had said that even in *Sheol* was the presence of God. Mark had read the words many times; but now, for the first time in his life, he was to be tested on whether he really believed them.

They were as ready as they would ever be, and

moved off down the incline – down rather than up because instinct said this would take them to the heart of things. As they progressed, anonymous forms hovered at the edge of the dim pool of illumination; each in turn proving harmless if unfamiliar.

The entrance slipped away behind, and Mark increased the power to the lights accordingly. Saatchi at the rear side-stepped periodically to sweep the beam of her spotlight back the way they had come. At the bottom, the shaft seemed to open into a formless void from which air drifted up that was even more oppressive and noticeably warmer. They reached the entrance. An incandescent line of crimson spiralled radially from the second cylinder in Paul's grip as he generated the shield; the transient stabilizing into a crimson ring about a metre in diameter. Mark turned the dial on the power pack round to the stop at maximum, and the chamber was transected by a blue-white beam.

As the light searched the darkness, the impression formed in Mark's mind that they were inside a long-dead carcass. Line upon line of wooden casing projected into the chamber from the walls, this shelving lined with innumerable rows of dusty volumes.

It was the skeleton of what had once been an underground library. Here and there, the light settled on an area that seemed to have decayed completely, as if some virus had concentrated its attack and produced total destruction. The wooden structures had been eaten away to leave gaping holes. Books lay stacked on the floor, forming low walls at odd angles to the regularity of the original design.

It was while inspecting one of these areas that the lights they were carrying flickered, steadied momentarily, then abruptly died.

They froze. All that held the darkness at bay was the dim illumination from the baraq in Paul's hand. From the pristine clarity given by the glare of the spotlight, forms were suddenly reduced to uncertain greyness.

Mark felt the icy coldness of fear reach out and touch him. He swivelled the voltage control but there was nothing. His fingers felt for the terminals but they still seemed secure.

'Just a second.' It was Saatchi. 'It's this one here. The lead's come adrift. She was tracing back along the second cable to find the other one; they had wound the two loosely together. Her fingers had just closed on the point where the two leads parted company, the one dangling freely, when the noise came to them through the darkness.

It began as a low and strangely choked rumble, then slipped sharply up the octaves to evaporate on a whispered high note. Paul moved to place himself between the direction of the sound and the other two.

'Hurry, Saatchi!' Mark's voice was low and urgent.

'I am! I am!' she replied. Her searching fingers found the plug at the end of the lead, then she fumbled and it slipped from her grasp. The sound came again, more insistently it seemed; and this time Mark was convinced that it came from no human throat.

'Got it!' she exclaimed, and brought the plug to the socket.

There was a sudden commotion in the direction Paul was facing, a determined scrambling of something moving in the darkness. Twin orbs that could only be eyes appeared at the end of the long passage they were now facing.

Mark felt his father brace himself and saw the eyes blink once then accelerate towards them with harrowing speed.

'Now, Saatchi! Now!' he cried.

Her fingers jiggling the plug at the socket found the correct orientation; the pins went home and there was a sudden flood of light on the floor. Mark swung his lamp up in an arc that met the approaching form an instant before it drew level with his father and the baraq, sweeping down towards it to deliver a blow midway between the eyes.

Just in time, Paul checked the trajectory, discharging the bolt over the head of the animal and into the darkness. Then there was a confused jumble of forms as Phoenix bounded into them.

The dog was overjoyed to be reunited with Saatchi and jumped up at her in a display of affection. It was some while before they could undo the tight bandages that swathed the dog's head and securely muzzled her. This was what had prevented them from recognizing the sounds she had struggled to make as Saatchi's scent came to her across the room. But who had confined her and tended the wound on her crown remained to be seen.

They moved forwards cautiously, investigating each recess in turn, and it was in the fourth that they made the discovery they had been seeking.

Tanya was lying on a filthy litter, shrouded in jumbled, tattered blankets. They stumbled over the debris to where she lay and Paul knelt down to examine her. The shield devolved and he replaced the cylinder in his belt.

The bedding drawn about her was rank and coarse. She appeared to be sleeping and he felt for a pulse along her neck. There was an ominous pallor to her complexion, but her skin was warm to the touch.

'She's alive,' he said finally. 'Either asleep or sedated. I don't know who did this,' he indicated the bandaged shoulder and arm, '. . . but I'd say we have something to thank them for. They must have patched her up after the crash.'

Saatchi knelt down beside her and touched her cheek as if checking for warmth. 'Poor Tanya. I wonder what happened?'

They watched over her for some time, listening to her deep and regular breathing. She was indeed sleeping peacefully. At first they were too engrossed to notice that the smell that pervaded the room had suddenly grown stronger.

Then Mark commented quietly, 'I think we're about to find out what happened.'

The others turned and saw, some distance away, a figure standing watching them. It gestured in what might have been a shrug and spoke with no animosity.

'We did our best for your friend. She's improving slowly.'

They stared in astonishment at the speaker. Robed entirely from head to foot, there was no feature visible. The voice came from a black hessian mask completely covering the face and framed by heavy woollen cowls. The hands were lost among the folds of a ragged cloak reaching almost to the floor. Feet and legs were bound in shapeless wrappings that rendered footsteps silent. Paul recognized now what he had seen at a distance and dimly in the shop two nights before; one of the Dark Ones.

'Your curiosity is understandable I suppose,' the figure said tiredly, 'but I think it's unfair to be subjected to this kind of scrutiny. Would you mind, please, dimming the light and pointing it in some other direction?'

Mark set the light down reluctantly and edged himself out of the shoulder harness to put the power source beside it. He tilted the beam upwards to reflect off the ceiling and put Saatchi's spotlight along the wall.

'Thank you,' the Dark One said gratefully. 'We are a little – reticent – about our appearance. I'm afraid there isn't much to see.' It took a step forwards, then hesitated. 'Please put away your weapons; they make me nervous. There is no need, I assure you.'

Saatchi spoke up. 'We don't mean you any harm; we've come for our friends. Why did you take my dog?'

'I am sorry she was ever taken from you; but we had no choice in that,' the Dark One replied. 'We had no idea who you were or what you were doing here, and could not risk being discovered. As things turned out, it was inevitable anyway. Events seem to have overtaken us rather rapidly. Still, your dog is well, and has recovered from the regrettable way in which we were forced to silence her.'

'What have you done with the bounty hunter?' Mark questioned suspiciously.

'Ah . . .' the other paused. 'The man of violence. Unharmed – but uncomfortable. We must decide what to do with him later. Which of course depends largely on him. It is unfortunate he now knows about this place. We are worried if we let him go . . .' the voice trailed off rather than express the fear that they would be hunted down and killed.

Other silent forms were emerging from the gloom, coming forward and flanking their representative; faceless masks turned upon the new intruders, who found themselves scrutinized like some rare species. Such variety and perfection of human form had not been seen for many years. Mark edged closer to the others. They had no idea who these people were, or what they wanted of them; and he wasn't sure he wanted to find out.

Paul counted seventeen. He stood up and addressed them generally.

'Who are you? And where do you come from?'

Another answered. 'We are the ones who were left. We haven't come from anywhere. We've always been here.'

'Survived the war and the killings,' another continued. 'When we saw what was happening to the

80

survivors, the others like us, we made sure we weren't found.'

'The funeral pyres burned for weeks,' another commented blandly.

'What happened to Tanya?' Saatchi asked.

'We found her, unconscious, by the side of the road where she jumped from the car. We had seen the chase and the final explosion at the far end of the street. She was badly hurt and lying in the open where she would have been found. But we reached her first and brought her back here. It seemed there was no threat; not like the other one. We knew he would have to be dealt with, and took the precaution of removing a little something from his vehicle when he left it unguarded. We realized from the dog that there were more of you, and that he wouldn't go away; so we acted to prevent more violence. His sort is safe only in captivity.'

'But now you must tell us why you are here,' another continued. 'Your friend was not very coherent, but it seems you are making for the prison-camp. If that is so, then we must try and dissuade you.'

'We have relatives there,' Paul explained. 'We have come to free them.'

The first one they had met laughed quietly and without mirth, shaking his head at their apparent naïvety.

'There is no escape from such a place, apart from death,' he asserted. 'Before you leave, we will tell you about the prison-camp, and perhaps then you will choose a more sensible course of action.'

19

Saatchi was inspecting the bump on Phoenix's head and enjoying the attentive company of the dog again. It was true, the injury was slight and the girl's spirits were higher than they had been for some time; unaccountably so really, since they were still no nearer their original objective of finding Natasha and Ghia. But for the moment it was enough to have Phoenix back, and she was loving the dog uninhibitedly.

'You seem good companions.' A woman's voice made her turn and she found one of the Dark Ones nearby watching them, but from a respectful distance.

Saatchi tried to smile. 'We've been through a lot together; maybe even everything. We were found together in the first place, and Phoenix wouldn't be separated from me.'

'Found?' the other inquired gently.

'Yes. It is strange, isn't it?' Saatchi agreed with what she took to be mild surprise in the other's tone. 'I'd been abandoned on the fringe of the green belt. One of the planters discovered us and took us home. When they realized we were marked,' – she avoided the more usual term – 'they hid us. And brought us up.'

'You were very young then – when you were found.'

'About six.' Saatchi paused and tilted her head. Then, with a trace of suspicion, 'Why did you ask that?'

'Oh; because it's a terrible thing; to be left. Especially when too young to remember your parents. I just wondered how old you were.'

Saatchi was unsure what to say next, and continued to stroke the dog affectionately, hoping vaguely that the stranger would go away; but she didn't.

'Umm. You said you were *marked*. Didn't they notice when you were growing up? I should have thought it would be quite difficult . . .'

Saatchi explained. 'Not really; it's only my eyes. I wore lenses all the time.'

'Ah; I see.' This explanation seemed to satisfy. 'It's your − left − eye particularly, is it?' the point was pressed further.

'Yes,' Saatchi replied, embarrassed and self-conscious. 'I'm surprised you can see at all in this light,' she wondered out loud. And then she said, 'Look, don't think I'm being funny − but why are you asking me all these questions?'

The Dark One hesitated and her cloaked hand moved up towards her face doubtingly before settling back beneath the folds. She seemed agitated and stumbled for a reply.

'Well, it's . . . I wondered whether . . .' She gave up, and then spilled out another request hurriedly, 'I'm sorry, but I need to know; you haven't got a brother, have you?'

Saatchi stood up and faced the woman. 'Yes, I have,' she said simply. 'Now I think it's time you told me who you are.'

The woman appeared about to take flight, and hovered uncertainly. Then she replied quietly,

'I'm a friend of your mother.'

Saatchi stood her ground firmly, although she was deeply shocked. This unexpected admission stood alone for several moments before the other continued.

'We were all above ground − your mother and two

children, and one or two others. The killings had finished, the Empire had gone, and we were left. We survived by scavenging for eighteen months; the supermarkets were stocked full of tinned goods and there was still some animal and plantlife surviving. Then two of us . . . became ill, and joined the survivors underground. It was a voluntary isolation you see. To avoid passing it on.

'We still met on occasions. Your mother used to talk of making the journey back to the cities. It was still fairly easy to get in then; the boundaries weren't so tightly drawn. Political tension was easing; patrols were becoming less frequent. And then they started developing the green belt. It was an ideal opportunity – lots of civilians moving back and forth between the very fringes of badlands and the city. She decided the time was right.

'I saw her just before she left. We sent her with as many provisions as she could carry. She went. And that was the last we knew. Until seeing you.' She halted temporarily, then went on, 'I thought you might be the child grown up. I was curious; about whether it was you, why you were here, what happened to your brother.'

'I've come back to find him,' Saatchi replied. 'He was taken by the Sentinels. That much I do remember.'

The shrouded figure swayed slightly and the voice came back incredulously. 'Taken? In the camp? But she said she was taking you to the green belt; it's in the opposite direction. I don't see . . .'

'I was the only one who was found,' Saatchi asserted. 'Maybe the others were both taken together.'

'No. It's not possible.' The woman seemed distraught. 'I watched them set out.' Then she seemed to check herself and continued in a calmer tone. 'We were sure she got away with the children to safety. All these years we've believed.' She lapsed into silence.

Eventually Saatchi tried to say something consoling.

'You must have been very good friends; I can see she meant a lot to you.'

'We were very close,' the other replied, and Saatchi could tell that it was tearfully. 'I wouldn't have trusted anyone else . . .' She faltered. 'In those days, I mean. People were desperate. But we went through it all together.' She seemed to be talking absent-mindedly and then excused herself. 'I think I will go and sit down for a while with my friends.'

Saatchi made as if to question her. What did she mean, that she 'wouldn't have trusted anyone else'? With what, for goodness sake? Her explanation didn't hold water. She had been going to say something else, then changed her mind. Or maybe she had caught herself in time would be nearer the truth.

The woman stalled a little weakly. 'I'll come and talk to you again, soon. After a little rest.'

And she was already backing away.

Paul faced Devo across the table. 'They'll let you go, you know. But they're worried you might tell the authorities.'

Devo was toying with the cigarette lighter, and now looked up to meet Paul's gaze. 'Now why should I do that?' he said disgustedly.'They've got it bad enough already without those punks busting in here to finish the job off. What do they take me for anyway?' He shifted irritably in his seat. 'Stinking hole. I'd like to take this dung heap and tell the Commissioner precisely where he can . . . Anyway,' he turned cynical, 'what's the use . . . ?' His thoughts came back to number one. 'So you think they'll let me out?'

Paul was surprised at this brief expression of disgust that was a glimpse of decency in the other. And the fact that it was so unexpected made him realize how completely he'd written him off. He had been wrong to dismiss him so readily.

'I know they will,' Paul replied.

'And you found out what you wanted to know?'

'Yes.' He wouldn't betray the survivors, he was sure of that.

'Then this little chat's over.'

Paul rose to leave, and then the other added, 'Incidentally, what are you here for? I know the girl's after her brother. But how about you?'

'My wife.'

'Then who's the other one — the one in the car?'

'Her twin sister.'

The mercenary grinned. 'Now, you don't expect me to believe that?'

'I don't really care,' Paul replied evenly.

Devo shrugged. 'Well, I suppose I hope you find her. Anyhow, I won't get in your way.'

Paul was again surprised by his response. 'I didn't expect you to,' he said. Having previously held one another in what could only be described as contempt, it was strange to find themselves parting on a note of tentative and mutual respect.

They were almost ready to move. After first trying to dissuade them, the Dark Ones had relented and provided them with the information they needed — the location of Omega 4. Tanya was still groggy, but they were taking the stretcher so she could rest as necessary without slowing them down. The medical supplies and food were staying behind.

Paul was talking to the one they had first met. It was hard to understand why, but the Dark Ones were resolute in their refusal to go with them.

'We must remain here,' he asserted obstinately. 'If we go, the disease goes with us. If we stay it dies here with us.'

'There may be a way,' Paul insisted.

'You are a rash and foolish man,' the other said in rebuke. 'There is no cure. We're victims. Can't you understand?' he concluded despairingly. 'We haven't got any hope; we don't want any. It's easier that way. That's how it was with the first one, and that's how it will be with the last.' He spelt out the message in single evenly spaced words: 'It's what we are.'

Paul couldn't think of a single new argument. He turned away, and went back to the others to load up.

Saatchi was in another part of the underground complex, talking to the woman again, who was holding something out to her that she had long despaired of seeing.

'It's a photograph. Here. Of your mother.' She dropped the small print into the transparent plastic bag taken from the medical kit and Saatchi sealed the top. She looked at it closely. It was so strange that she should find it here of all places. And stranger still to think that the camp might hold *two* members of her family.

'I don't know what to say,' Saatchi replied, looking up, 'except thank you. I only wish I could give you something in exchange.' She slipped the picture into her jacket pocket, then smoothed back her hair before shouldering the back pack. As she did so, one of her fingers touched the fine chain around her neck, and an idea occurred to her. She reached up and undid the clasp.

Holding it out to the other, she said, 'Here, take this. It's all I have left from that time, except for Phoenix. I'd like you to have it.'

The silver chain hung from her hand and upcurled fingers. The other put out a mittened paw to take the weight of the stone. Saatchi flinched at the sight of the misshapen hand, then turned her wrist to allow the chain to slip from her grasp. It cascaded silver onto the outstretched palm and then the hand closed around it and withdrew beneath the folds of the gown.

'Thank you,' the woman said peaceably. 'You have made me very happy.'

Saatchi stared in bewilderment at the faceless mask, and found herself crying. It was too much to bear that she should say that and mean it.

'I wish there was something . . .' she struggled.

'It's enough,' the other reassured her.

Saatchi shook her head angrily. 'No, it *isn't*. It isn't enough at all. We're leaving you here and it's so pathetic. We can't take two and leave twenty behind. It's no good. It isn't.'

She turned away, flushed and tearful. When the sound of her own sobs subsided she realized there was still the sound of crying.

The Dark One had moved back into the shadows and turned towards the wall. Through the layers of cladding, strangely muffled, came a pitiful snuffling that reached down inside Saatchi, seized her spirit and wrung from it a cry so intense that to silence it would have been a kind of death. Then she had crossed the space between them and was hugging the other one close, and words were pouring from her mouth that her lips could not recognize nor her mind understand.

After many minutes, she released the woman and stumbled back, fumbling at the shelves for support. She was trembling with weakness, drained of emotion, and studied the dirt that streaked her skin and clothes dispassionately, aware that she had done the unthinkable, embraced the untouchable. But somehow the realization seemed to have no impact; there was nothing left.

The woman was still standing, face to the wall, when she turned and left to find the others. And clutched in her concealed hand, the Dark One held the simple stone and silver chain. Her deadened fingertips played absently at her neck, and fumbled again with the crude necklace hidden there and the two knot-marked gaps it contained. One of the stones had been returned.

They retraced their steps up the long sloping tunnel towards the shaft of light at the exit. Standing on one side beneath the opening to the outside world was a heavily-cloaked figure, a lone representative to make the last farewell. Between them, they helped Tanya to the surface and then followed one by one. As if by chance, Saatchi was the last to leave. As she moved forward to climb the rubble staircase, the stranger leant forwards and restrained her with a whisper.

'Wait.'

She stopped, surprised that the other had approached so closely; normally they drew back.

'Yes?'

'I have a message for you.'

'Oh?' She gazed vaguely in the other's direction,

almost used to the anonymity by now, expecting to see nothing.

The voice spoke again, calmly and unhurriedly. 'It is this.'

Suddenly she was listening very hard for the words that were to follow:

'*The fabric of this world wears thin. The kingdom is breaking through. We are of the final dimension.*'

The words had a familiar ring, as if she had dreamed them before and now they had become real. But she hardly noticed them. They registered, but her attention was on the speaker, her curiosity roused. This one was different; hadn't shied away, didn't have that quality of hopelessness that pervaded the others' speech – sounded altogether too assured. But even as she pondered, the figure moved back and began to descend the tunnel. She raised her voice urgently.

'Wait: I don't understand. Why are you telling me this?'

'Because you have already begun,' the figure replied. 'You *have* broken through. Understand what is happening. And tell others.'

Continuing on his way, the stranger was merging almost with the shadows.

'Where are you going? Come with us!' she called spontaneously.

'I have another message,' the voice came faintly. And she thought she heard, 'For another friend.'

'Anything wrong?' Mark called down.

She looked back down the passage and then up to his face at the lip of the opening. 'No; nothing wrong,' she replied mechanically. But the strangeness nagged her. Then she gathered her thoughts. 'I'm coming up.'

22

The road north was easy and they made good time. The task of carrying Tanya was organized as a rota: front, back and rest; front, back and rest. When they came to the junction where they were due to turn, they stopped for a while. The camp should be less than a mile away.

Mark eased his back pack to the ground and stretched, then looked round. Saatchi was standing with her back to him a few feet away, looking across the road, perfectly still, head tilted back. He looked beyond her in the direction of her gaze and stared up at the solid, strong spire towering over them, planted as a signpost on their route.

Saatchi turned towards him, blanched, and looked down the avenue leading westwards. What she saw was a small child, wandering inquisitively in the middle of the road, too engrossed in his search to notice something silent, unmoving among the shadows. Something that had come soundlessly to life, and separated itself from the darkness. She felt again the sensation of being gagged, the feel of the warning cry choked in her throat by fear. She saw the little boy turn, his expression full of horror, and catch her eyes once through the intervening form as she shrank back against the wall. Ghia had fallen in a faint to the floor and disappeared.

'This is the place,' she whispered to Mark as he

came to stand beside her. 'This is where it happened. The Sentinel was behind . . .'

He moved to place himself between her and the sight that was generating the fear.

'You aren't alone, now,' he said gently. 'This time will put it right. You don't need to be frightened by memories.'

'It's all right,' she said, and then glanced up at the sky, now heavily clouded over. A dark grey mass was drifting steadily in their direction.

'Looks like a storm,' she commented.

'Mmm,' Paul agreed. 'It was miles over to the west when we first came up, but it's definitely coming our way, and building up too.' Right on cue, they clearly heard the first and distant sound of thunder.

Paul was examining some equipment from the back pack he had been carrying. He hurriedly dismantled the apparatus — three snap-on attachments encasing the cylinder of the baraq — and replaced each part in its corresponding compartment of a small, solid case which he then returned to the pack. He seemed preoccupied and the others left him to his own thoughts.

Mark knew something of what the baraq could do. It had vanquished the metal hounds of Titan two years earlier, and saved his father's life many times before. He wondered at the thought that its power should need enhancing — he presumed that to be the purpose of the three attachments. What manner of foe would demand such recognition? What exactly were they coming against in the Sentinels of Omega 4?

Tanya was gaining strength rapidly and felt able to walk for a while. Her shoulder and arm were still painful, but she was keen not to be a hindrance. Mark was eager to press on. Both he and Saatchi seemed to have weathered well the rigours of the past two days.

Looking back towards the city and its spires, Paul

voiced the thought for them all, 'I don't like turning my back on them.'

'I don't see what else we could do,' Mark said, 'if they wouldn't come with us.'

'There should be something,' his father replied. 'It's all so hopeless.'

'They've convinced themselves,' Tanya concluded.

'They almost convinced me,' Paul retorted. 'That's what bothers me.'

Saatchi shook the hair back from her eyes and looked at them quizzically.

'What did you make of the one by the entrance? He seemed different to me — I thought he might come.'

Paul and Mark exchanged blank looks.

'What do you mean; the one by the entrance?' Mark asked curiously. 'I didn't see anyone.'

Saatchi half laughed. 'Oh come on, don't be silly — you must have seen . . .' Her words trailed away and the smile died on her lips as it registered that they hadn't the faintest idea what she was talking about. They really were clueless.

'Paul — didn't you . . .?' she faltered. He shook his head. 'Tanya?'

'I was too busy trying to get up that rubble heap without falling over,' she replied. 'I didn't notice anyone; but I wasn't really looking.'

'Why don't you just tell us what you thought you saw?' Paul asked gently, aware that she was becoming increasingly puzzled.

'I didn't *think* anything,' she said. 'I actually talked to him. He said,' — she quoted — ' "the kingdom is breaking through". He said I'd broken through. I didn't know what he meant.'

She stopped.

Paul was staring down at the ground. After some time he looked up at her, and his expression was strangely serious.

'Saatchi,' he said quietly. 'What *exactly* happened when you went off talking to that woman?'

She was taken aback by his directness. 'Well I – well, nothing really,' she replied. 'At least, nothing . . .' but the explanation forming in her mind was never given, and the interruption meant that for some time she alone had an inkling of what was happening, what had been happening, and what exactly she had done.

Mark was staring back down the road. He had stepped out a couple of paces to see further, and commented, 'You're not going to believe this.'

Then they could all hear the approaching sound that had attracted his attention, and Saatchi's explanation was lost.

The car drew level and a hatch opened. They watched Devo non-committally.

He grimaced. 'Thought you might need some help,' he offered defensively.

'From you?' Paul was surprised, but stirred.

The mercenary grinned and shrugged. 'Nobody else around,' he said.

Paul looked long and hard at the ground before catching his eye again. 'Why the sudden change of heart?'

Devo winced in embarrassment; admissions didn't come easy. 'Let's say I don't like to see someone get a raw deal.' He paused. 'I never imagined the commissioner and his friends were Snow White and the seven dwarves, but what we saw back there was kind of graphic, if you know what I mean. I figure he deserves one in the eye from them. And since they aren't about to accept offers of help, and I reckon what you're going to do will get right up his nose – I thought I'd offer my services. Free. Just so you know what a really nice guy I am.' He grinned smugly. 'Take it or leave it. Me – I'd say you need the assistance.'

There was a long drawn-out silence, during which

they each made up their separate minds. At the end of it, Tanya spoke for them.

'I think your offer's accepted,' she levelled. And then added, her voice softening, 'With thanks.'

They slung the gear in the back of the car where they had previously been imprisoned, and then joined Devo up front. Inside was all comfort and high tech; a very seductive vehicle. When the compartment was sealed, the bounty hunter half turned to Paul beside him.

'They call me Devo. I think I know the way.'

Then they were moving fast towards the final confrontation.

They had left the car near the end of the street where the houses petered out, and were walking up the gentle incline to the bridge ahead. The factory on their left was silent now and eerily empty; much more noticeably so than the terraced rows they were leaving behind. Probably because there was a greater expectation of sound and industry, if only the background whoosh of extractor fans.

The canal was stagnant, unhealthy, its stench drifting up to them on the afternoon breeze as they passed over. More buildings on their right and they were onto the railway bridge. Paul signalled to them to wait and moved forwards cautiously to see over the crest of the road. They saw him lift the binoculars to his eyes and scan the countryside.

Four railway lines passing obliquely beneath the bridge and branching into sidings curved in a gentle arc round to the left past some outlying buildings at the approach to the station a mile to the south.

With dusk approaching, it was time for a small cluster of lights to announce the station's night-time presence. But, like the solitary railway signal standing guard over the tracks, they would fail in their duty and fade themselves into the encroaching greyness.

In the opposite direction the tracks led away to the north. The ground rose on the far side of the rails in a bank running in a parallel direction, the crest of the ridge ten or fifteen feet higher than the level of the railway. Just beyond, a line of regularly placed tree trunks with splintered boughs defined the edge of the meadow, and through their rotted members he could see the goal of their mission.

The low ground adjoining the railway lines would conceal themselves and their vehicle; the bank between them and the plain was a natural rampart. Behind it they were invisible, and from its raised vantage point they would mount their attack.

Paul lowered the glasses and glanced around one more time. It was to be the scene of his last battle; he knew the Lord was telling him that. With Natasha safe, it would be time to rest, and to pass on the mantle to another's shoulders. A new generation was being equipped for service, called by the same voice to cross swords with evil and to overcome. He thought of Saatchi, who moved in realms unseen almost without realizing, and of Mark. He knew the boy felt the same fire in his soul, the burning spirit of God's heart. He would not rest as wickedness prospered. Paul recognized in his son a warrior in the making. It was to Mark and Saatchi that the victories of tomorrow belonged. As for today – the privilege was his, and his the promise of this finest hour. He turned back to the others, his spirit rising to the challenge, and silently reaffirmed his acceptance of the honour.

24

Port Meadow stretched away into the distance much as it had done for more than a thousand years. In the middle distance the river wound its way lazily across the plateau from right to left, a grey streak smudged on the brown of mud and scattered turf on which the camp stood.

'Explains why Tanya couldn't find an exact location,' Paul muttered to Mark who was lying beside him on the low earthbank. 'Looks like they follow the work around.'

Again he swept his gaze over Omega 4 – a jumbled collection of khaki tents and prefabs settled near the centre of the open plain. There was an appalling poverty in the fabric of the camp. Every part of its structure was stamped with the mark of expendability. It had cost little to establish and less to maintain. When something wore out or fell apart, the population usually shrank to match the reduced accommodation. It was near the end of its life with maybe a handful of inmates.

The only thing of permanence was a solid central block from which a short radio mast rose. This was the heart of the camp; the link with the outside world, the core of its intelligence. The computer it contained established the regime of the camp through the unopposed rule of the Sentinels.

The Empire was efficient; that much was plain. Establish a camp, fill it with slaves, rule through machines whose loyalty was unquestionable, and you could reclaim the land for just the price of lives whose value in the first place was only in the labour they could provide. Set up such camps all across the country and the contamination and dissidents would take care of one another. Eventually the badlands would yield crops to supplement the produce from the green belt to the south.

A movement caught Paul's eye. He glimpsed a prisoner emerge briefly from one of the containers before taking shelter again. Two of the Sentinels stood motionless, strange parodies of the human form, wildly disfigured, monstrously large. Any move against the camp would bring an instant response, a ruthless execution of their orders to repel any attack. The Sentinels would fight to the death, whatever meaning that might have for such as they. He lowered the binoculars.

There was nothing to alleviate the dolour of the scene, which was uniformly drab, the darkening sky leaching out what colour there was.

'If we don't move quickly, we're going to have problems with the weather,' Paul said as he belly-shuffled back down the bank, and the two of them went over to report back to the others.

They had the map on the ground, weighted with stones.

'There's a second bridge here,' Tanya pointed out. 'Over the canal. There should be some cover. If we use heavy fire to draw the Sentinels over in this direction and into the open, you could pick them off with cross-fire from over there, Paul, before they realize what's going on. It's a perfect sniper's position. And if they want to come and get you, they'll have to split two ways.' She paused. 'Can you get the radio mast with the first shot? The camp has to be isolated as the first move to stop a distress signal getting out. Otherwise we'll have heaven knows how much Empire firepower breathing down our necks.'

'I could,' Paul replied, 'but I thought we just agreed I was to lie low until you draw the Sentinels out; if I fire first, they're more likely to get a rough fix on my position.'

'Mmm. You're right.' She looked across at Devo. 'How about you?'

'At a conservative estimate,' he feigned calculation, 'I'd say I couldn't miss.'

'That's what I call a healthy ego,' said Mark.

The remaining details were quickly settled. Mark would go with his father and take a transceiver for communications from their end. The others would stay put. Tanya would have the second set and be the other half of the link.

Saatchi would man the radar in the vehicle, just in case any signal got out of the camp and summoned up airborne support. She also had the beacon which was their lifeline to safety. It was the final detail. High above the Earth, in a stationary orbit over northern Europe, a tiny communications shuttle was waiting patiently for activation. Left behind by the spacecraft that had brought Paul and Mark from Ekklesia, it was ready to depart, on receipt of their signal, and reappear from hyperspace over Ekklesia to relay their pick-up call. Waiting in readiness on the launch pad was the rescue ship that would be despatched to bring them back to safety. Saatchi must switch on the beacon as soon as the camp was taken. They must make sure at their end that the pick-up was clean and easy if they were to evade pursuit.

The moment came for Paul and Mark to depart.

Suddenly they realized that they were to face the final trial divided. The radio link would not make up for the fact that they would be effectively cut off from one another, about a quarter of a mile apart. Just at that moment, it didn't seem like such a good idea and Paul wondered whether they were doing the right thing. But it did look as if it doubled their chances and the Sentinels would be caught in crossfire on open ground. He reasoned it through again, and it still seemed like the best decision.

Mark was talking to Saatchi. Paul went over to where Tanya was sitting with the map and the radio, a little apart from the others.

'Goodbye time again,' she smiled.

'Hmm. Yes, so it seems,' he said, kneeling beside her. 'How's your shoulder?'

'It'll do. How do you feel?'

He looked her in the eye then away and at their surroundings.

'I'm ready. If I didn't think we could take those things on and beat them I wouldn't be here. I've seen what this can do with the extras they provided,' he tapped the baraq, 'and frankly, it scares me. They wouldn't have allowed me to come if they weren't sure it was enough. All the same, I'd rather it was already over.'

Mark and Saatchi joined them, and Phoenix pushed into the tight circle of friends as they sat down on the earth. They drifted from conversation into prayer and finally into silence. At last Paul seemed to come to a decision.

'I know it feels as if we're in the front line here, and I suppose in a way we are,' he admitted. 'But let's remember we aren't the only ones who want to see this job done. The Lord is with us all the way. It's his battle; it always has been.' He looked around the circle. 'Let's go for it.'

Devo was some way off, busy with some equipment. He looked up as Paul and Mark came over to him.

'We're leaving,' Paul said, although it was obvious. 'I wanted to tell you we're glad to have you with us.'

'The pleasure's mine,' the mercenary replied, and Paul was half inclined to believe it. But he'd been wrong before.

'We'll see you later.'

'Sure you will. I'm not going anywhere.'

They left. Tanya walked with them some distance up the road and watched them for a while as they made their way north to the second bridge over the canal. Then she rejoined the others and began to concentrate on her duties. She estimated twenty minutes for them to get into position.

The mercenary had assembled a heavy duty laser on a small tripod on the crest of the ridge and was connecting up power cables leading back to the car. Tanya watched him with a cold feeling. Those skills had so recently been used to the Empire's benefit and perhaps would be again. He was enjoying the preparation, totally immersed in the weapon. It was more than a little morbid. Her eyes followed him as he went back over to and swung into the vehicle and the driving seat next to Saatchi.

The systems check ran smoothly. He relaxed and looked at his watch; they still had another ten minutes or so before the others were ready. He started a new smoke and watched Saatchi at the radar display.

'Everything working okay?'

She nodded: 'It's fine.'

He leaned over and indicated a row of switches on the counter measures console. 'If anything untoward shows on that screen, flip these and give me a yell, then get out,' he instructed. 'This one here's a multiple imager; makes us look like five targets strung out in a line. These three,' he moved along the row, 'are full defence routines, set up in serial loop; they just keep going round till you turn 'em off or the whole lot's a pile of dust. These,' – indicating the last few – 'are something special.' He grinned. 'More than enough to make this the centre of the action while we fade away elsewhere.'

'You must have done a lot of killing in your time,' she said, taking in the machine's capabilities.

'More than some; less than others,' he replied matter-of-factly. 'Don't expect it to end here, either.'

She gave him a hard, searching look. 'You know what they say; "live by the sword, die by the sword". Unless you change, your days are numbered.'

'They're numbered anyhow,' he pointed out accurately. 'And then again, maybe you shouldn't believe all people say. Far as I know, only the first half of that saying is true for sure.'

'You know, I don't think I've ever met anyone with fewer ideals spread more thinly than you,' Saatchi said with some humour.

'In that case, I could show you a whole lot of life,' he concluded. 'You think I'm bad; you should meet some of my friends. In fact, if my attentions weren't elsewhere at the moment, I'd recommend it. I think you'd be surprised.' He broke off suddenly and exclaimed, 'What's all that about?'

A noise was coming from the camp, sounding uncomfortably like an alarm. They baled out of the car and went over to Tanya who was in touch with the others over the radio.

'Mark tripped off a sensor,' she explained. 'Went straight through it without realizing. They want to know if we can see what's happening; they're still on the road side of the bridge and can't see a thing.'

Devo was already crawling up the mud bank to take a look.

Saatchi indicated she wanted and got the transceiver. 'At the moment, they probably think it's a lone scavenger,' she told Paul at the other end. 'One of the Sentinels will come out to take you in. If it doesn't find anything, it'll track you till it does. You've got to get clear and let them take Mark.'

The mercenary was back. 'One of those things is moving in their direction,' he confirmed breathlessly, 'And moving faster than I'd have thought for its size.'

Tanya took the handset. 'Paul; get out of there!' she half shouted into the mouthpiece. 'Mark will be all right for a while. The Sentinel will take him into the camp and we'll still have some time.' She waited for a return transmission what seemed an age, conscious every second of the Sentinel closing in with its crude but rapid bipedal gait.

'All right. I'm falling back,' Paul's voice came. 'But you'd better be right about no immediate danger.'

'Why do they make those machines so ugly?' Devo commented as he watched Mark being marched into the camp.

'Lack of imagination,' Saatchi replied, taking the glasses for a look. 'And I don't suppose they spend much on making things look nice.' She watched Mark disappear into one of the larger tents, and tried to make out what the activity of the Sentinels signified. Their

103

half-human gestures seemed all the more obscene when she remembered what they were.

Tanya was still talking to Paul over the radio. 'I don't think they know anyone else is out here; otherwise there'd be a lot more happening. So the next thing is that they'll question him to try and find out where he's come from. They're predictable enough. It's one disadvantage of having a totally automated system. Since he'll resist, they'll probably go to stage one synthesis to try and break him. He should come through that okay; it usually takes four or five sessions, though I can't say it's pleasant. If we can move before they start, it would be easier on him.'

Paul's voice came back. 'I'm going as fast as I can. The first trap was almost impossible to spot, and I've got through a couple more now; but I'm still not close enough. It could be another half hour.'

'All right. Let me know,' she replied. 'It's going to start getting dark sometime in the next hour; and I don't think the rain will hold off much longer.'

'Okay,' he agreed, and the set went dead.

Thunder was echoing regularly across the landscape now, and they had each felt one or two drops of rain already. There was no shelter to be had from the fractured stumps of deadwood that passed for trees round about, and if the storm did break, they were in for a drenching. Tanya bit her nails impatiently, and shifted to try and relieve the ache in her shoulder. She felt slightly woozy, but it was hard to tell whether it was the painkillers or the fact that they were wearing off. The pain was mounting steadily and beginning to weigh heavily on her spirits.

'Come on, Paul,' she muttered irritably. 'Come on.'

Saatchi was still spying on the camp through the glasses.

'Something's happening,' she said. 'They're transferring Mark to the main building.'

'That means they're starting already,' Tanya voiced dejectedly.

'He will be all right, won't he?' Saatchi asked. 'I mean; there's no danger of any long-lasting effects from whatever they're going to do?'

'He'll be all right,' Tanya assured. 'Really; I mean it.'

Mark found himself facing a second door as the first closed behind him. Adrenalin was pumping round his body and he was strangely dizzy for a moment. The room seemed to fade, as if he was about to faint, and he caught a brief snatch of an old melody as if heard over a radio somewhere in another room. In a few seconds the music faded. Then the door opened onto a large room, about the size of a small sports hall. He stepped in, and the entrance closed behind him.

He was alone, the Sentinels having remained outside. It was a relief; their touch had been nauseous. His new environment seemed harmless enough – panelled wood floor and walls, a row of high windows on three sides up to the ceiling, and dark glass panels on the fourth, all out of reach. The lighting was less than clinical; functional really. All in all, he decided, this must be the soft approach.

Having checked out the room, he leaned back against the wall to see what would happen next, and tried to relax. He wondered about the others, particularly Saatchi for some reason. No sooner had the thought entered his head, than the door by which he had entered opened again, and she stepped into the room.

'Saatchi!' he exclaimed, coming away from the wall to meet her in the centre of the room, 'What happened? No . . .' He caught himself and gestured silence. 'Don't tell me; they're bound to be listening.'

'Actually, we already know why you are here.'

The voice startled Mark. He looked round for the speaker, but there was no obvious source. It seemed to be right next to him. An illusion, he decided; to disorient him. All part of the process probably.

Saatchi was pacing the room, checking the solidity of the walls. She seemed remarkably calm.

'I didn't expect to find you in here,' she commented as an aside while continuing her inspection. Then she came back over to him. 'Have they told you what they want?'

Mark was slightly taken aback. Hadn't she seen him be transferred? Surely the others had been watching?

'Why don't you look at the glass panels?' the voice suggested. It was still disconcerting, even though Mark knew what was going on. Must be hidden loudspeakers somewhere.

He turned in time to see that the ebony windows were fading to transparency. Behind them were two smallish cubicles, and in each was a silent observer. The first, he knew immediately, was his mother; and he guessed and saw from Saatchi's reaction that the second was her brother.

Mark and Saatchi walked over to look up at them, and the others looked down, pressed against the glass but hopelessly imprisoned. To see Natasha at last, after all these years, made his heart leap. She was Tanya's twin, to be sure; just a little weathered by comparison. It was incredible how she had survived.

There must be a way to get to her. Mark looked round for something to climb on, to raise him up to the level where he might smash through the window. A question began to nudge his consciousness as he tried to think what to do. Why had he and Saatchi been left alone together in the room? They didn't expect to get anything out of them from sheer boredom did they?

'We'd like you to tell us a little about your background,' the voice suggested coaxingly. 'Start wherever you like; there's plenty of time.'

Mark and Saatchi exchanged glances. 'I'm not telling you anything,' he replied coolly.

The inquisitor laughed gently and mockingly. Why a woman's voice? Actually, now he thought about it, it seemed more indeterminate.

'Don't think I don't admire your resolution,' the voice flattered him. 'It's just that so many of our conversations start that way; it's a bit of a cliché you see. But I think you'll find it hard to surprise me.' The tone was very smug and gently condescending. They stayed silent.

'I expect you're wondering what all this is about,' the voice went on. 'Well, it's very simple really. You see, *I* am interested in finding out about you; and *you* are naturally reticent to tell me. That being the case, we have to arrange for you to be more amenable, to avoid wasting everybody's time.' There was a pause.

'Why don't you open the door in the wall behind you?'

Mark turned and was surprised to see a small section of the panel with a recessed handle at about shoulder height. He obviously had not checked carefully enough the first time round.

The door opened and he took out the small gun inside the small recess behind it.

'What do you expect me to do with this?' he inquired sarcastically, checking it was loaded.

'Oh, probably nothing. It's just one of several options,' the voice replied. 'This is what they are. First, you can tell us as much as we want to know, and then all four of you can leave here safely. In which case, the gun is irrelevant.

'Second, you can use it on your companion. In which case she will be spared whatever else we might have in mind to try and persuade you. If that is what you decide upon, then you should also know that in the event of your killing her, one of the hostages you can see will also die; although we aren't going to say which one. In this way, we retain an element of chance in the game.

'Third, you can use it on yourself. Again, one of the hostages will die. There is nothing to stop you combining the second and third options.

'Fourth, and final, option: you do nothing at all. In which case the other three will die in some order at our discretion, and − this has been decided − you will be the last to go.'

Mark looked down at the gun. The idea of using it was simply ridiculous. He thought back to the vows he had taken just a few days earlier − to preserve life and not to take it − and the years of training before that, and knew they were going to have to do a lot better than this to break him. He was still a long way ahead.

'You're crazy,' Mark muttered.

'The rules of the game might seem harsh,' the voice admitted, 'but there is one way you can win. All you have to do is tell us about yourself; it needn't incriminate anyone else. After a while we will probably be satisfied, and all this will have seemed unnecessary. Some have chosen that option; your mother for example.'

'You're lying,' he asserted.

'There's no point in our lying,' the voice came back. 'Just think about it; how else would your mother have survived? We have told you all the options. What do you deduce from the fact that she is alive and well? Of course, it might have been a different game, with more choices; but I don't think so.'

'*What is this?*' Mark was thinking. '*What's going on here?*' He was starting to be drawn in; wanted to answer back. But he fought the impulse.

'I see you aren't convinced. Then why not ask me a question?' the interrogator went on pragmatically.

'Choose something you think it most unlikely she would have told us.'

Mark hesitated. He didn't want to play the game at all. He wasn't about to begin some type of mental hide and seek with these people. Who *was* he talking to anyway? He turned to Saatchi. 'Ignore it. We don't need much time.'

'I see you entertain thoughts of rescue,' the voice was amused. 'Don't expect any help from the others. The outcome depends entirely on you yourselves – and us.'

Mark was jolted. The thought of rescue had been hardly formed and they had known. For a moment, he felt suspended. He groped at something that had just almost surfaced from his subconscious; like part of a dream on waking. Something . . . But Saatchi distracted him.

'Tell them something, Mark.'

'What?'

'Tell them something.' She shrugged matter-of-factly. 'Anything. If you don't they'll kill us.'

Her attitude surprised him. Normally he'd be inclined to go along with her suggestions because she usually made sense. But this was much too compliant.

'That doesn't sound like you,' he countered. 'Can't you see what they're trying to do? I'm not about to accept boundaries just because they want me to believe they're there. We *aren't* beyond help.'

'Then what are we going to do, Mark?' she asked.

'Nothing,' he said. 'Nothing at all.'

She looked up at him, perfectly calm. 'The fourth option.' He dropped the gun, and they held one another.

'They can't touch us,' he whispered, and it was a prayer.

They stared into one another's eyes. She never

flinched as he scrutinized her deformity. Since birth she had been marked, her left iris shot through with a violet – he shuddered mentally and looked at her again, and the blow knocked him sideways.

'Your eyes,' he said quietly, with the feeling of suspension returning.

'What?'

'Your *eyes*,' he said definitely. 'I remembered them wrong; carelessly.'

Floodgates opened and the realization was a wall of water sweeping all before it. He remembered the overheard conversation between Saatchi and the Dark One: an auditory memory – the woman had said it was the *left* eye. And it was Saatchi *remembered* as she stood before him: a visual memory – but flawed; wrong. This time the *right* eye. The two memories clashed in his consciousness; there was no way they could be put together. Non-superimposable mirror images.

What stood before him was not Saatchi; it was his memory of Saatchi. And as he watched, in final proof, the truth asserted itself. The right eye became normal, the left became flawed.

The synthesis had failed.

From the moment of dizziness, and the snatched memory of a song from years ago, accidentally dislodged as the mechanism scanned his mind, he had been living a dream. He had been in some drug-induced state that rendered him pliable to the synthesis constructed in his subconscious.

And as in the moment a dreamer realizes he is dreaming he suddenly awakes, Mark found himself recoiling from the illusion around him. The room dissolved, he was falling through nothingness, and all that remained was *I am*. And then that too was swallowed up by the void.

26

Tanya rolled over in the mud and closed her eyes against the pouring rain. She heard the shot and the laser sizzled, steam rising from the heatsink. When she rolled back to take a look, the aerial had gone and the camp was cut off.

The gun fired twice again and she watched the first of the Sentinels go down. It was hard to follow the action through the field glasses, because the visibility was so bad.

'Got that one before his shields went up,' the mercenary commented. 'The others might not be so easy. Anyway, they're coming this way all four.'

He aimed again and the weapon shrieked violence against the oncoming foe.

He swore. 'Have to make some adjustments here to get some more kick,' he grunted. He ran for the car and returned clutching a small piece of electronics which connected into the gun mechanism. He tapped a few keys and read off some figures, then whipped out the leads and discarded the unit.

'Okay, let's see where that gets us,' he muttered to himself. Same energy; more power, shorter pulse. He sighted the leading figure and fired again, jerked his head back and winced in the steam. The Sentinels were still approaching.

'Did you miss?' Tanya asked.

He gave her a searing look. 'A direct hit and not so much as a dent. Whatever your friend's got had better . . .' The remainder of his sentence was lost in a crackling roll of thunder as the sky overhead lit up. He swore again, reached for the unit, and plugged it in again.

Tanya could hardly see through the rain, a solid wall emptying from the clouds above. An agonizing shock of pain shot across her shoulder and down her arm, making her flinch and cry out. She clutched onto the transceiver handset and shouted into it, 'We're in trouble here, Paul. Do something, quickly!'

The reply came an instant later, a flash across the meadow brighter than the lightning; one of the Sentinels crumpled.

'That's some gismo he's got there.'

The mercenary was impressed, looking up temporarily to inspect the carnage. Then he was back at the task of reprogramming the laser mechanism.

'How far now?' he yelled over to Tanya above the sound of the storm.

'Fifty yards!' she shouted back.

'How many?'

'Two,' she yelled. 'One's gone after Paul.'

He commented drily, under his breath, and unplugged the unit again. Then he looked across at her and all the brashness was gone. Suddenly she felt cold. Had she said something . . .?

'Only one shot,' he explained, staring at her intently before looking down to the gun. 'This'll fuse everything. It's the only way to get enough power.'

She wiped a greasy wet lock of hair away from her eyes and was still for a time, stunned. Then she looked back over the plain. Both figures advancing towards them were now cut off from Paul's line of sight. There was nothing he could do to help them. She dropped the radio and it rolled into a puddle.

She slithered down the bank and splashed her way through the mudpools over to the vehicle, and leant against the wet metal, the rain trickling down over her face. Away in the trees there was a final volley, a shower of sparks and a yell of pain. Then the mercenary rolled into the quagmire, extricated himself and staggered in their direction.

Devo was three-quarters of the way to them when the world lit up and a strand of live power twisted its way to earth not a hundred yards away. They felt, rather than heard the thunder; it shook the ground, the air and their bodies with a raw violence that threatened worse. It made him fall momentarily, then he was up and made it to the vehicle.

They saw the flash of Paul's baraq again and Tanya whispered to herself, 'He's okay. He's going to make it.'

'Get in the car!' the mercenary yelled; and then he caught sight of Tanya's expression and turned.

Standing astride the embankment, and turning in their direction, was the last remaining Sentinel.

'I don't believe it. No,' Tanya whispered. 'This isn't going to happen.'

Devo tried to look away and couldn't. He had expected to be repelled, but the combination of human flesh and machine was more repugnant than he could ever have imagined. The gene factories had spawned a monstrosity against nature. Human tissue had embraced mechanism in a search for the ultimate survivor in a place where what lived, died; and what was dead to begin with, rotted. This thing, half-dead, half-alive was the solution they had found. A Sentinel might live forever.

Devo turned away and his head lolled against the wall of the vehicle, his mouth dribbling sputum down the surface. '*This is it*,' he thought. '*This is really it*.'

Tanya was backing away slowly, mesmerized. Saatchi clambered out of the car . . . and found herself

113

looking into the face of her wildest nightmare. Her eyes snapped shut. She felt the cold wetness of metal on her back and realized she was shrinking along the side of the vehicle as her legs tried to carry her backwards. The rain driving in great heavy drops against her closed eyelids trickled in rivulets down her face and neck. She fought for breath in the face of the wind.

'*Even wind and sea obey him . . .*'

She flinched as the lightning flashed and the thunder struck her ears, reverberations ringing in her head with a pure high note. And over the clear bell-like tone, the sounds of the storm suddenly distanced, came the words:

'*My authority I have given to you.*'

Her eyes opened and she stretched out her arm so that the span of her hand covered the Sentinel visible between her outstretched fingertips. She held it there, and began to add her voice to the storm, speaking a fluent tongue of no earthly origin, the language of her youth given by the spirit of God.

From the corner of his eye, Devo saw her standing in what seemed to be symbolic resistance, her arm outstretched as if to keep the Sentinel at bay. He recognized her guts for not running, but his was a different course of action.

Devo reached into the cabin and his fingers closed on the handle of a small, light weapon. Then he turned and took a couple of steps away from the vehicle and out into the open. He had always thought he would die in the company of rogues, on some disreputable mission, at the hands of those as ruthless as himself but for once more clever. It seemed things had turned out differently; not much consolation, but he recognized that something inside him preferred it this way.

It was coming forwards, the part that might have been a face turned steadily towards him, tracking his movements. The arm muscles bulged and a hand

114

clenched, sinews parting and sliding over vitreous metal.

There was a flurry at Devo's feet and something slipped past; ugly dog racing headlong against its opponent. It leapt – and he admired its timing – and the jaws snapped closed on metal throat in what should have been the death grip. He flinched as the beast somersaulted sideways, swept carelessly aside by an iron hand.

Saatchi shouted something unintelligible and from the corner of his eye Devo thought he saw her about to imitate Phoenix by repeating the useless self-sacrifice. But he was going to get there first.

He rushed the Sentinel; as far as it was possible to rush in ankle-deep mud. Two shots found their mark and glanced off impotently, then his shoulder crunched into the metal torso, and he strained to heave it off balance. Something smashed down from above, and he was on the ground, and staring up into the face of death against the heavens. He whispered a plea so quiet that none could hear it.

The Sentinel raised its fist and in so doing completed the image of opposing forces clashing face to face between Saatchi's outstretched fingers and its own curled knuckles. The girl flung a climactic declaration into the heavens. Her words, as if carried by the ionic vortex streaming upwards, met in the belly of the clouds and drew down from above the answering bolt that split the sky. Tearing the heavens, the might of Another's hand flashed in the lightning. The contorted aether licked a tongue of fire over the upraised arm of the Sentinel before invading the rest of its metallic body, seeking the earth at its feet. For a moment Devo was bathed in an unearthly light. And when he opened his eyes again, the image had been shattered, the leviathan was no more.

Towering over him was hell's executioner, its gaze

fixed upon him from burnt-out sockets, a fallen champion upon whom sentence had been passed. As he lay, unable to move, the arm still raised for the blow swung suddenly down under its weight. And behind the hand pointing towards him, the death's head grinned '*I'll get you yet*'.

In that instant he knew that his reprieve was temporary. The forces of darkness that he had courted so long had sought to claim him, his life the price for his failure and their humiliation. He had dealt in death, and now death had come looking for him. And time was on its side.

Saatchi lowered her arm and slumped against the car. It bore in upon her numbed consciousness that somehow her faith had overcome. The power had come from on high. But the faith to exercise that power, to take authority had come from within.

'*I have given you authority over all the power of the enemy.*'

The words were true, and she would never forget them. She reached into the car, took hold of the beacon lying on the console and slid back the protective panel. She depressed the button beneath and a light winked on for a second as the signal went out. Help was on its way.

Saatchi was kneeling over the mangled body of her dog, bending so low that her hair covered the animal's face. There were strange noises in its throat and its eyes

116

seemed not to see her. Tanya splashed over and tugged at her shoulder.

'Come on. They'll be here soon.' The beacon had sounded; rescue was fast approaching. They had to be ready.

'I can't leave her like this.'

Tanya glanced down at the animal, and her feelings wavered, but there was no time. 'We can't wait,' she insisted. 'I'm sorry.'

She tugged more forcibly and called over to Devo. Then, between them, they dragged Saatchi away and into the car. It rose from the ground, turned and accelerated away from the scene of the conflict, out across the meadow to the camp and the others.

Paul was marshalling people into an area at one end of the camp. The rain was whipping across the plain, driven by a cold wind. The prisoners were bewildered and frightened, and Paul was desperate to make himself heard.

A woman fought her way to the edge of the crowd and made her way towards him. Her windswept hair obscured her face, and tattered clothing flapped wildly in the storm. Bare feet slipped in the mud and she put out an arm to balance. He reached across and caught the hand and their fingers entwined.

So steadied, she was free to catch back the dishevelled locks flung across her features. From the shadow of the hand which shielded her eyes from the gale she looked across at him and he saw in her gaze the flash of recognition. For long moments they looked, reminded perhaps of the time years before when a look had carried as much significance, but then of parting. Her lips formed words, and though the sounds were lost in the wind, he knew their meaning.

Suddenly she turned away and began to tug him in the direction of the largest building. A door set in the side yielded easily to the baraq and he clambered inside.

Mark lay on a narrow couch encased by an electronic chrysalis, silent now. His inert form remained entombed in the capsule in which the Sentinel had placed him at the start of the synthesis. From the jaw upwards, his head was contained within the mechanism of the scanners, the interface through which the computer had entered his mind. Paul searched the console, not designed for human hands, and prayed to find the right button. When he did, the sarcophagus opened and he lifted the body out. Mark was unconscious, but alive. A bolt from the baraq ensured that the synthesiser would serve the Empire no more. Then he took Mark outside, carried him over to where the car had stopped and lifted him into one of the leather seats. He turned away from Mark and surveyed the remnant of humanity that had served at Omega 4.

The sound of an aircraft rose above the wind and rain and he looked up for a sight of the ship. It came in low from the north, homing in on the beacon straight as a die, and touching down so close they could see the pilot on the flight deck.

Paul knew again how good it was to have such friends. Many people over the years had given thanks for those known as the Knights of the Church. How many lives had they saved, snatched from the Empire's hand? Paul had given the best part of his life; perhaps it was fitting that on this last mission he was the one to receive and be grateful.

The crowd moved forwards, groping towards the aircraft. Hatches swung open to receive them, and the prisoners surged forwards with a ragged momentum towards the gateway to freedom.

Paul's gaze swept the sky, though he doubted the ability of the Empire's defences to engage or track the rescue ship; the technology gap was too large, and the skill of the pilots too great. They would have flown at zero altitude on a scrambled flight path until the final approach. As such they would have been beyond detection, their destination beyond prediction.

Two figures detached themselves from the crowd and started over in the direction of the vehicle. Saatchi was supporting her brother's weight as he leaned against her, bewildered and bemused at what his senses were telling him. Captivity was all he could remember, and now it was at an end. He was almost shy of his sister, and sought the reassurance of Natasha's touch in the group of strangers. Paul recognized she was like a mother to the boy; indeed perhaps he thought she was. Paul knew she would have loved the orphan like the child she had lost. He looked down at Mark in time to see his eyes opening. Mark was tired and confused, but what he saw dispelled his fears. Too weak to speak, he was content to look into the face he had sometimes despaired of seeing. Natasha smiled down at the son she hadn't seen for eleven years, and his eyes returned the sentiment in her own. Then his eyelids drooped and he drifted back into sleep, secure in the knowledge that it was journey's end.

Paul's gaze travelled back to the landscape they were leaving behind; an unrelieved grey-brown vista stretching away to the horizon. He was about to look away when a movement caught his eye. Back where the last Sentinel had fallen, something was moving towards them. He knew a moment's panic, reached for the binoculars and lifted them to his eyes. He brought them into focus, and what he saw across the field sharpened to confront him.

'They're coming,' he whispered. And then they all heard him clearly, 'They're coming.'

Strung out across the expanse of land was a straggled line of survivors, wind tugging at their makeshift garb, leaning into the rain and struggling across the plain. Through the binoculars, in the foul weather, it was hard to distinguish forms, alike and amorphous as they were. But eventually Paul could hazard a head-count. They were all there. For some reason they had changed their mind. He wondered why. If it had been him, he doubted whether he would have been able to stay behind, with the certainty of what would follow, and allow the chance to escape to pass by. And however slim the hope of cure might be, it was preferable to none at all.

But they had been adamant in their decision to put an end to the illness through their own extinction, so that it died with them. Why were they now prepared to risk carrying it elsewhere? Saatchi and Tanya came out of the vehicle to look. He handed the binoculars to the girl and after a long look she passed them to Tanya. They watched in disbelief as the Dark Ones made their way towards them.

A quick look over his shoulder told Paul that the camp was almost evacuated, just a few people not yet on board. It was time to transfer Mark to the ship.

Saatchi beside him was fumbling in her jacket pocket for something. The packet came out covered in mud and she wiped the polythene clear. She stared hard at the photograph and then up at the figure leading the small band of people, closer now and with cowl caught back and trailing in the wind, face met directly by the elements. And in that instant she knew, quite clearly, what the stranger had meant. They had broken through, and she could hardly believe it. Then she was running across the muddy field towards the other, slipping in her haste on the slick surface.

Paul knelt to pick up the picture from where it had fallen, and Tanya handed him the binoculars. He raised them to his eyes and stared at the woman towards whom Saatchi was racing. It was the woman in the photograph. That was strange. Why had Saatchi got a picture of one of the Dark Ones? But even as his mind groped towards the answer he realized with a shock that there was something even more strange about the woman in black.

It was almost unbelievable. There was no trace of disfigurement; she was completely whole. He searched the woman's face through the binoculars and her complexion was smooth. Against the skin of her neck, a silver chain and string necklace entwined. The matching stones lay together. Mother and daughter were reunited.

He lowered the field glasses as Saatchi and her mother embraced. So that was it. That was what had changed their minds. He didn't know *when* it had happened, maybe when Saatchi was alone with her or maybe sometime since – could it have something to do with the stranger? – but it was transparently clear *what* had happened. Her mother had been healed. And the others had hope.

'Is it really true?' the girl asked, leaning back to look into the other's face while not letting go, clutching her through the rags. 'Do we really belong to one another?'

'It's true,' the other replied. 'You're mine just as much as the day we parted. I knew you couldn't remember,' she continued, 'when we were talking earlier. But I had to be careful – not to give it all away. I couldn't let you find out, because . . .' she faltered, 'because of the disease. I lied, you see. It was I who joined the Dark Ones, and my friend whom I entrusted with getting you to safety when she left for the green belt. Somehow Ghia must have wandered close to the camp and been taken.'

'Yes, I remember that,' Saatchi interrupted.

'And then she took you to safety. When I saw you today,' she went on, 'I had to lie, to spare you from knowing. It was better you thought I was dead.'

Saatchi was shaking with emotion. 'You didn't have to lie,' she said quietly. 'I would still have loved you, even as you were.'

Her mother smiled. 'I know that; because you did, you see. You loved me, without knowing who I was, because you touched me. I think that was it.' She seemed to come to some understanding without voicing what it was.

'That was it?' the girl repeated, searching the other's expression.

'Yes; I think that was how it happened.' She thought back; 'I think that's what he meant.'

Saatchi felt a surge of excitement. 'The stranger,' she said, half in exclamation, half questioning.

'Stranger? No, I don't think so,' her mother replied. 'He said he was your friend. At least he knew you well.'

Saatchi was eager, 'What else did he say?'

'Oh, I can't remember it all, there were so many things.' She looked suddenly into her daughter's eyes, 'But he told me you loved me. And he told me it was important; that there was hope because there was a faith that overcomes. And just before he left, he told me to look at myself.'

She held out her hand again and stared at it as Saatchi knew she must have done then, with wonder in her eyes. Saatchi felt she might cry. She looked round at the Dark Ones, huddled together against the rain a little way off, wanting to come closer and hear the story again, but reticent still, uncertain of whether their presence could really be bearable.

'We're glad you've come,' she raised her voice to carry over the foul weather. She looked towards the waiting rescue ship. 'Because . . .' her voice dropped so that only her mother heard, 'because it's time to go home.'

Paul had lifted Mark out of the car and was making his way with Natasha across the small stretch of land to where the others were boarding the plane. Some turned for a farewell glance, looking back over a lifetime of sweated labour, before disappearing inside. At the bottom of the ramp, a crew member took Mark from Paul and carried him inside. For the first time, he was free to embrace his wife.

Her face was shining. Paul tried to follow what she was saying and eventually she saw that he could not and gave up. She turned him to look out over the river to the far side, and for the first time he noticed a broad expanse of green stretching away into the distance. It was so utterly out of place, so completely unexpected that he doubted his eyes.

'See!' she exclaimed. 'This is what we've done. It's our land, Paul; all of it. We've bought it back. We've bought it back.' He looked at her, and for the first time he saw himself not as the conquering hero, rescuing the maiden in distress; but realized that all the while she had been building. Building a new countryside from the remains of the old.

He looked out over the new crops and realized that the land had been brought back from the very brink of ruin. The sweated labour of the exiles, banished to the badlands and interned in the camps, had turned back the tide of decay and devastation. They had rid the fields of their mantle of poison and restored the earth beneath. They would produce food once more.

'It's a breakthrough,' Natasha smiled. 'A real breakthrough. And it's only the beginning.'

28

Devo watched them board the craft: Paul and Natasha; Mark and Tanya; Saatchi with her mother and brother; the Dark Ones from the city; the interns from the camp. He watched it all, from the first to the last. He saw the hatches sealed, and he followed the craft with his eyes as it rose in the air.

That was some machine, he admitted. Part of him would have liked to have gone with them; just to learn. But he had other things on his mind. The cabin sealed and he turned on the power. He was a city boy; and that was where he was heading. But first, there was something he had to do.

The car touched down again at the edge of the meadow, and he got out and looked around till he found what he was looking for. Then he made his way over to the small red and brown heap lying by the edge of the embankment, hindquarters dipping in a pool of mud.

Phoenix's head lifted a little as she saw him coming, and she tried to get up in a way that hurt him to watch. He wiped the back of his hand across his mouth and reached inside his jacket. The gun was a lump of lead in his hand, and as he lifted the barrel, telling himself it was the only humane thing to do, he swore to himself that this was the hardest and the last killing of them all.

29

The return to the stars was journey's end for them all. Paul watched the grandeur of Ekklesia rising to meet them, and thought back over the days since they had been there before. Natasha was home at last, and Tanya too. Saatchi had found her family. He looked across at her, and for the life of him he couldn't see why she looked so sad. Emotional reaction? Anticlimax? He turned away and gave it no thought; they were almost there.

For Saatchi, it was true that there was an overwhelming joy at finding her brother and mother. It seemed selfish to feel any trace of sadness. But no one could deny that they had left one behind. One who had shared her life, and whose last act of loyalty had cost her own. Phoenix was dead. Her body on the battleground was all that remained to tell the tale of the assault on Omega 4.

Inside, amidst the joy, was a part of her that would never forget. And that part of Saatchi was weeping.

EPILOGUE

The room was dark, and the only sound was the steady breathing of the one asleep on the bed. The alarm was set for 6.30. He was accustomed to short hours of rest: rose early, worked long hours and returned to the bed late. Exhaustion was an occupational hazard.

The door buzzer was a long time in eliciting a response. He fumbled for the switch, groaned as the light hit his eyes, heaved himself to a sitting position and took a few deep breaths before making it to his feet. The clock said 1.05.

The sound died as he lifted the handset.

'Mmm . . .' was all he could manage. The voice at the other end of the line was quiet and urgent.

'It's Devo. I need help.'

He rubbed his eyes. 'Uh . . . help. Just a minute.' He pressed the button to admit his visitor, replaced the handset and went back into the bedroom for a dressing-gown. Then he made his way downstairs, along the corridor past surgery and waiting room to the small entrance hall where a shadowy figure stood in darkness.

'Leave it,' the other cautioned as his hand went towards the light switch.

'Suit yourself,' he shrugged. 'What can I do for you?'

'It's serious. I need surgery.' He was breathing

heavily, the other noticed, as if he was carrying a large weight. Suspicions stirred.

'Are you running?'

'I'm running.'

He thought for a moment then turned and led the way. 'Come on through.'

A door led off the corridor to a flight of stairs down to the basement. The room flooded with light. At the bottom of the stairs the doctor turned to his patient.

'What on earth!' he exclaimed. 'Is this some kind of a joke?'

Devo placed the animal on the operating table and then looked the other in the eye.

'It's no joke.'

The other swore. 'You get me up in the middle of the night for a dog? I'm a doctor, not a vet. Get that thing out of here.'

Devo waited for him to cool down, and wiped some of the blood off his hands in the meantime. When he had quietened down, he said coolly, 'I want you to reconsider.'

'You want me to risk my neck for an animal?'

'That's right.'

He went across and looked the dog over, viewing its wounds with some disgust. 'Look – can't you take it somewhere else?'

'I'm running,' Devo replied. 'There is no somewhere else. You know that.' The other seemed to be wavering. 'You owe me,' Devo pushed.

'I know,' was the defensive reply, then, 'Look; *if* I do it – *if*, mind you – then,' he paused as if measuring up the task, 'it's going to cost you.'

Devo was past patience. 'If that's what we're talking about,' he said coolly, reaching into his jacket, 'I want you to know that it'll cost a lot more if you don't.' And he could tell by the other's expression that the gun in his hand made the point. But even as the other gave way

127

and agreed, a small voice that Devo couldn't quite silence said that this time he was bluffing; that the threat was empty. And deep down inside, he knew the voice was right.